ROYAL BOROUGH OF GREENWICH

Follow us on twitter

Eltham Centre
Archery Road, SE9 1HA
Tel: 0203 915 4347
Renewal line: 01527 852384

KT-495-267

Please return by the last date shown

E1 7/22		

Thank you! To renew, please contact any
Royal Greenwich library or renew online or by phone
www.better.org.uk/greenwichlibraries
24hr renewal line 01527 852385

This book is dedicated to all the amazing children out there who did their best to stay kind and keep going, even when the world seemed a bit dark. You absolutely rock, every single one of you.
R. D.

STRIPES PUBLISHING LIMITED
An imprint of the Little Tiger Group
1 Coda Studios, 189 Munster Road, London SW6 6AW

Imported into the EEA by Penguin Random House Ireland,
Morrison Chambers, 32 Nassau Street, Dublin D02 YH68

www.littletiger.co.uk

A paperback original
First published in Great Britain in 2022
Text © Rachel Delahaye, 2022
Illustrations © George Ermos, 2022

ISBN: 978-1-78895-315-3

FSC
MIX
Paper from
responsible sources
FSC® C020471
www.fsc.org

The Forest Stewardship Council® (FSC®) is a global, not-for-profit organization dedicated to the
promotion of responsible forest management worldwide. FSC defines standards based on agreed principles
for responsible forest stewardship that are supported by environmental, social, and economic stakeholders.
To learn more, visit www.fsc.org

2 4 6 8 10 9 7 5 3 1

MORT THE MEEK

AND THE
MONSTROUS
QUEST

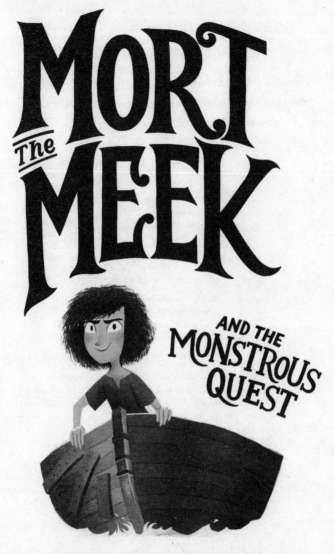

RACHEL DELAHAYE
ILLUSTRATED BY GEORGE ERMOS

LITTLE TIGER
LONDON

DEAR UNFORTUNATE READERS
– A WARNING

This is not your average tale. This is not a jolly page-turner before bedtime. Oh no – it's definitely not that. This is a story that swims through a world of weirdness without armbands, and not everyone has the stomach, eyes and teeth for such a thing. If you don't have the stomach, eyes and teeth for such a thing, then leave now.

Are you still here?

All right, let's try again...

DEAR UNFORTUNATE READERS WHO HAVE THE STOMACH, EYES AND TEETH FOR SUCH A THING...

This tale contains no fewer than **FOUR** trips to sea, a barrage of *SLIMY* insults and some seriously **TORMENTED** characters. If you get seasick, or if you're nice, or if you'd rather not discover the dark side of human nature, I advise you to leave now.

Are you *still* here?

Then you're mad. Mad as a kipper's slippers. And you'll probably enjoy this horrible story. Read on, but let's start at the real Chapter I.

THERE WERE SIGNS

"What's beautiful?"

"A sunken treasure ship."

"Why is a sunken treasure ship beautiful?"

"Oh, I thought you said booty-full."

There were signs. Signs were there. Were there signs...?

(This chapter is called **THERE WERE SIGNS**, so what do you think?)

In fact, there were **LOADS** of signs. They were on every wall, pillar and roof. On every raven that stood still long enough for someone to stick a piece of paper to it (and there were quite a few). Brutalia was covered in the things and they all said:

Citizens of Beautiful Brutalia,
Gather in the square tonight for some news.
Your Divine Queen

Well! The citizens of Beautiful Brutalia fell backwards in shock for two reasons:

I. The signs were scented – they wafted sweet smells as they flapped in the wind (or on ravens) and people had never sniffed 'sweet' before. The island reeked of rot. And the only perfume available was **Eau de Errr**, sold by perfumer Olfa Smelch in buckets (although he called them boutiques) called *Olfa Smelch Smells* (and he really did).

2. The Queen's orders were normally belched door to door by one of the Queen's guards, not written down. But weirder than that was the word **BEAUTIFUL**. People rolled the strange word round in their mouths until it got all spitty, and they were as baffled as bath plugs on the moon.

You see, it's hard to explain beautiful to those who have only ever known grime, grunge and grot, and lots of other horrid things beginning with 'g'. Because life on Brutalia could never be beautiful. Have you been there? If you have, I'm surprised you're not missing three toes and an earlobe. If you haven't been there before, then hold on to your churning guts because

~~WELCOME TO~~ BAD LUCK, YOU'RE IN BRUTALIA.

Brutalia was a spiky island in the Salty Sea that attracted precisely no one. Its reputation was cruel, its jagged coastline skewered sailors quicker than a kebab and there was a **rotten stink** that clung to it like mist on a bog. The rotten stink was actually a *cloud of despair* (a key ingredient of **Eau de Errr**). And despair was always there – in the air, in your hair, under there, *everywhere*. No sailor with a brain or a nose would stop for the night. Not unless they wanted a visit to hell.

Because that's what Brutalia was: **hellish.**

Beneath the island's raven-infested watchtowers, in a single city brimming with filth, Brutalians fought. They fought for food; they fought to survive; they fought to feel alive. Even Brutalia's littlest kids lived for a punch-up. They roamed the streets in gangs, offering tooth removal, using the traditional method of Fist-to-Face.

Who could possibly let them live like this! I hear you cry.

I'll tell you who – the Queen and King of Brutalia. And they were royally revolting.

The King was a bit smelly, but it was the Queen who was the real stinker. She had the compassion of a brick. She loved no one and cared for nothing – and if she had known about the King's secret pet cockroach, Corky, she'd have killed him without batting her stick-on beetle-leg eyelashes. That's the kind of person she was.

So you see, explaining the word *beautiful* to a Brutalian was like trying to describe a new colour or a new taste. But there it was, on all those signs: **Beautiful.**

Sweet smells, pretty signs, strange words... Something fishy was going on in Brutalia. Was it good fishy or bad fishy? The people would have to go to the square to find out. And they would also have to go to the square because that's what the Queen had ordered. If they didn't, they'd end up getting the **Punishment of the Day**.

But we're getting sidetracked now, and you don't want to get sidetracked in Brutalia or you might end up down a dark alley getting your teeth knocked out by a bunch of rascals.

(Told you there was nothing nice about this place.)

CHAPTER TWO
GOD, REALLY?

"Do you believe in God, Larry?"

"Of course I do. I saw him.
Quite big, rubbery lips, fins..."

"Are you sure you're not thinking of Cod?"

The square was packed and the royal procession out in full, complete with cooks, servants and royal pets. These were *official* pets, such as manky-breath tigers and giant lizards on leads (and definitely not Corky, the King's secret cockroach). The Queen had even brought out her Grot Bears. They were grotesque, bear-like creatures with small brains and big paws and they were present for one reason: to make the crowd behave. If these beasts were let loose, there'd be all sorts of trouble.

Depending on what sort of Grot Bear got hold of you – a loving one or a fighting one – you'd either be bear-hugged and crushed to death or ripped apart. Also to death.

Guards held up *QUIET NOW* signs, although at the sight of the Grot Bears an uneasy silence had already fallen over the square. The only noise was the revolting slurp of Grot Bears trying to lick their own eyeballs, and the occasional growl of a manky-breath tiger.

On a high stage in the middle of the square, the

Queen was helped up on to her long-legged chair, the seat of which was up a ladder and padded with ten cushions.

"Behold your God!" she said.

Being so high up, her voice was faint and no one heard a thing. Not even the guards below, who were too far away to kick. She plucked a megaphone from her skirts and tried again.

"Behold your God!" she shouted and raised her arms to the sky.

Confused, everyone looked up, spotted a seagull and guessed they should play along. "We worship you, oh seagull," they mumbled.

"**ME**, you imbeciles. **ME!**" the Queen shrieked. The seagull plopped something sticky on her shoulder and the air was thick with awkwardness.

The guards quickly held up signs that said *CHEER NOW*. The people did as they were told and hurrahed enthusiastically. Everyone apart from Mort Canal, the plumber's son. With his father, brother and sister missing at sea, he couldn't have produced a hooray even if he'd wanted to. Not even a little one.

"Try!" urged Weed Millet, the baker's son, who was Mort's best friend.

"*Hu-urgh...*"

"That's not a cheer – that's a ticket straight to the dungeons. Quick, get behind me."

The Queen no longer carried out executions, but she was still hugely keen on locking people in small dark spaces infested with rats, and she always sent spies into the crowd to root out disobedient subjects. Weed stood in front of Mort to hide him and cheered extra loudly for both of them.

Despite the huge chorus of forced cheers, the Queen began waving her arms and shouting, **"Come on! Praise me, you despicable worms!"**

"*She's totally off her rocker!*" Mort whispered.

Weed turned and nodded. "*Totally barking,*" he mouthed back, before Weed's mother shoved dough balls in their mouths. Whispering, mouthing, sometimes even breathing – the Queen could make anything punishable by the **Punishment of the Day** if she felt like it. And the punishment was clearly written on a chalkboard in the square.

PUNISHMENT OF THE DAY

HORNET PANTS
*Scream in agony as you are lowered into
underwear lined with the Queen's royal hornets*
please note: screaming is punishable by...

JELLYFISH PANTS
*Scream in agony as you are lowered into
underwear lined with the Queen's royal jellyfish*
please note: screaming is punishable by...

CACTUS PANTS
*Scream in agony as you are lowered into
underwear lined with the Queen's royal cactus...*
(You get the picture.)

"Yes, my loyal subjects, it's true. An old document found in the palace vaults has revealed that I am not mortal, like the rest of you snivelling losers. I am, in fact, descended from **GODS**. Actual **GODS**!"

The guards raised *CLAP NOW* signs and everyone obeyed, of course. The Queen smiled languidly, waiting for the clapping to die down. It took a while – no one wanted to be the first to stop; no one wanted to try on those hornet pants for size. When she'd had enough glory and was certain that every citizen's hands were red raw with effort, she beckoned to the guards to lower the signs.

"And SO..." she started. But the clapping continued. "Oi, you! Punished!"

One guard had fallen asleep, still holding up his *CLAP NOW* sign, and Enot Stone, the Chief Guard, marched him off to have his hornet pants fitted.

Annoyed that her big moment had been spoiled, the Queen's face flushed plum-purple and she yelled:

"LISTEN TO ME, YOU SNOT-WEASELS!"

The crowd fell deadly silent, as if wasps had landed on their lips (which gave the Queen a good idea for the next **Punishment of the Day**).

"You may wish to know why there is fancy writing and sweet smells all over our island. It's because everything about me from now on will be DIVINE. And you will all worship me as a God AND a Queen."

"We worship you, God AND Queen," the crowd mumbled.

"Excellent. Louder next time or I'll have you all barbecued. But there's another matter I must address. You, my *darling*, must go."

She spat out *darling* like you'd spit out a dead fly, and her bony finger pointed to the King, who was seated at the bottom of her high chair. He pulled himself to his feet with a groan, a belch and a small sob.

"Sorry, *darling*," she continued snippily, not sounding sorry at all. "Another document was discovered in the vaults, and it proves YOU are descended from a **Dank Empire**. Scribe Pockle, tell us all what **DANK** means."

The Royal Keeper of Birth Certificates and Legal Documents stepped forward with his dictionary. "Dank means disagreeable, dark and damp."

"YUK!" shouted the crowd.

The Queen seemed pleased. "Oh, King... When we married, I thought you were a noble posho. But it turns out you're closer to Corky than you are to me. Yes, I do know about your pet and I've squished him."

The King tried so hard to hold back his tears that he let go of something else.

FWARP!

"Don't start with your revolting noises," the Queen snapped. "It won't do any good. At the end of the day, I am a God and you are a Slob."

She snapped her fingers and Enot Stone led him away. Where the King was being taken nobody knew, not even Enot, who just dumped him round the back of the palace and told him not go anywhere.

The Queen cast her eyes over the crowd, which made them feel very uncomfortable. But not as uncomfortable as the three pairs of children she had stacked beneath the chair legs to raise her even higher.

"What am I?" she yelled.

"The Queen," replied the crowd. And then, brains clicking into gear, they shouted a confusion of alternatives: "A God? No, a Queeny God? A Queenish God? A Godly Queen thing? A Quod?"

"Oh, shut it, will you! It's God Queen. **GOD QUEEN**. And giving me your rancid adoration isn't going to be enough. So, what can you give me...?"

"I've got a carrot in the shape of an onion you can 'ave!" shouted Sally McRoot, soup maker and big fan of vegetables. "And I've got an onion in the shape of a potato. And I've got a couple of potatoes in the shape of bums."

The crowd hooted and hollered.

"I've got a bum in the shape of a bum!" shouted someone naughty in the throng and the square erupted in snorts.

Usually hilarity would be punished, but it gave the Queen a really handy segue* to her next point.

*Pronounced seg-way, this is something that offers an easy link to the next idea.

"If I wanted something from Brutalia, I'd take it and I wouldn't even have to ask," she sneered. "I own it all. Your homes, your children, even your backsides are mine. No, I want something from distant shores and forgotten lands. A trophy from a perilous adventure. And you're going to get it for me."

"Who, me?" said Sally McRoot.

"No, not you, cabbage brain," the Queen tutted. "By YOU, I mean anyone bold enough to take one of my fleet into the Salty Sea and bring back the finest of trophies. You will set out in teams of two and there will be a prize for the best trophy. A magnificent prize..."

She raised her arms and paused, making sure that

every ear was on high alert. As it happened, plenty of ears were on alert, including our hero's. Mort didn't care for God Queens or prizes, but the Queen had said, "take one of my fleet into the Salty Sea" and an idea was forming.

"The prize is this: I shall make the winners ... Demi-Gods!"

"What? Out of carrots?" said Sally McRoot.

"Out of papier mâché?" asked Fibris Peel, paper maker.

"Out of dough?" added Weed Millet.

Mort nudged his friend with a sharp elbow. "Shh. Any moment now, she's going to snap, you can be sure of it."

"Can you make a Demi-God out of pigeon poo?"

The Queen craned her head towards the giggling pigeon-keeper, Stubber Peckitall.

The square was so silent, you could hear a carrot drop.

"JELLYFISH PANTS!" she thundered. "Followed by **CACTUS PANTS**, followed by three rounds in the boxing ring with Warren, my least favourite tiger."

Stubber Peckitall was led away, wishing that he'd kept his pigeon-poo joke to himself.

"Next person to speak, I'll have their earlobes for earrings!" the Queen screamed. "Those of you who wish to sail, meet at the docks first thing tomorrow morning."

"Ha ha, you just spoke," giggled a very silly guard.

He was dragged away, obviously, and then the royal procession prepared to leave the square, which required everyone to bow very low.

Unfortunately Looby Larkspit (Brutalia's only comedian) bowed so low she startled a lizard, which set off the tigers, which set off the Grot Bears and made everyone very nervous. But after that hiccup they were gone, and the people left in the square breathed a big sigh of relief.

Then the chatting started, and the gossip began about the Queen's godly expedition. The Queen – a God! Who'd have thought it? Who among them would seek trophies and claim glory? Who would stay to keep Brutalia running? Who didn't care and just wanted to get down to the market in time for the good carrots?

"Are you going?" Mort asked Weed.

Weed grinned and bounced on his feet. "You bet. Anything to get out of another day of baking!"

"Then I'll be your team-mate," Mort said. "I'm going too."

"But ... but it's not like you to chase fame and status, Mort!" Weed said, surprised. "Not like you at all!"

"I'm not chasing fame and status, Weed. I'm going to look for treasure."

"But it's not like you to chase gold and riches, Mort. Not like you at all!"

"It's not that kind of treasure, Weed. I'm going to find my family."

CHAPTER THREE
HOPE CLINGS
LIKE A LIMPET

"Fancy a game of SNAP?"

"How about a lobstacle course!"

"What's a lobstacle course?"

"It's where we clam-ber over things."

"Nice one, Bruce."

Mort's mother wept dramatically as they walked to the docks in the dismal dawn light, clinging tightly to her son's arm. She wasn't taking it well. The Salty Sea was dastardly. "Do you have to go?" she wailed.

"Yes, Mum. They're giving us boats. Proper boats. This is a real chance for me to find Dad and the twins."

"Nah, they're gone, love," she sighed. She pulled a fork from her pocket and tested the prongs against her nose. "It's been two weeks since they got swept off a rock, chiselling limpets for tea. They'll be fish food by now. Or eel food. Or shark food. Or starfish food. Or—"

"Mum, please stop saying that! We don't know for sure they're dead. They could be bobbing around out there, waiting for help."

"Doubt it."

"Clinging to a piece of wreckage, living off seaweed."

"Unlikely, love."

"Or perhaps they've been rescued by passing sailors..."

"Look, I'm not gonna waste my energy being optimistic, and neither should you."

Mort looked his mum right in the eye. Well, both of them. They had lost their sparkle since half the Canal family had disappeared.

"Mum, I'm not giving up. I'm going and you can't stop me."

"No, no, **NO!**" she howled.

"I'll be fine, Mum," Mort said soothingly. "If something goes wrong, I'll find a way to survive."

"That's not it," she sighed.

"I'll take extra food so I won't get any of those vitamin-deficiency diseases."

"THAT'S NOT IT!" she wailed.

"If you're worried about sea monsters, I've got a small knife, even though using it is totally against my pacifist principles."

"THAT'S NOT IIIIIIIIT!" she shrieked, apparently inconsolable. Globules of water trembled on her lower eyelids.

Mort gently brushed a bug from her cheek before it got tangled in her tears. "Well, if you're not worried about drowning or poor nutrition or sea monsters, then what **are** you fretting about?"

She looked at him with streaming eyes.
Her bottom lip wobbled.

"Tell me, Mum. Tell me!" Mort pleaded.

Avon searched for the right words... Then she
found them:

"Who's gonna help me chuck forks?"

It hit Mort in the guts like a disappointing
sandwich. His mum had given up on his dad and
the twins and – whether it was grief or just plain
beef – she was now throwing all her energy,
and cutlery, into ding-dongs with the next-door
neighbours. (She only had one arm due to a terrible
jousting accident and was always after extra pairs of
hands.) The fight between the houses was an ongoing
feud and no one remembered how it started.

"I want to chuck forks at those slimy snot rags so
badly. And I need you to help me."

"But I'm against fighting, remember?"

"Oh yeah," she tutted. "Hopeless. Off you go
then, Mort the Meek."

He wasn't called Mort the Meek for nothing.

(Which is another way of saying he was definitely called it for something.) Meek means gentle, and that's what Mort was, and he was proud of it. In fact, he was the founder of the **Pacifist Society of Brutalia**, which had one and a half members. Mort was the one, and the half was Weed, who couldn't earn his full membership badge until he gave up fighting for fun at the vegetable market. (And, if you think there's nothing violent about vegetable markets, you've obviously never been hit by a knobbly turnip.)

"I've got an idea, Mum," Mort said, looking into her big blue eyes. She stared back into his average-sized green ones expectantly. "Why don't you try being meek while I'm gone? And NOT fighting the neighbours?"

"No can do. That woman called me a slug-bum yesterday."

Mort saw her fingers, face and toes start to twitch. An attack of fork-filled aggression was coming on. He thought quickly. "I have a plan. You tell the neighbours I'm going to the Salty Sea and coming back with a brilliant trophy so the Queen will make me a Demi-God. That will make *you* the *mother of a Demi-God*. They won't dare call you a frog-bum ever again."

"They called me a *frog*-bum? **FROG-BUM!**" she screamed. "When? Behind my back...?" Avon fell silent as Mort's words sank in. "Mother of a Demi-God. Oh, that's good, Mort! So you're risking your life just for me?"

Mort, who didn't want to go over the real reason again, smiled and nodded. Sometimes it was easier that way.

"You're gonna need all your strength. You're as daft as a cod's nostril when it comes to stuff like peril. Here, take this roasted rat for your journey."

Mort shrank back from the stained cloth package. "For the last time – I'm a vegetarian!" he said. (It wouldn't be the last time.)

There was a sudden slapping sound as the flat feet of Weed Millet beat against the wet cobbles. He skidded to a halt in front of them.

"All right, Mort?" he panted. "Oh hello, Mrs Canal. Is that a rat you've got there?"

"No." When Mort turned it down, Avon had bagsied it for herself. "Um, it's a stone."

"A lucky stone! Thanks, Mrs Canal. We're going to need all the luck we can get." Weed grabbed the package and it squished between his fingers. There was an awkward silence, until a raven overhead squawked and broke it, and Weed returned the unfortunate parcel.

Mort decided it was time to go. "Come on, Weed. If we don't leave now, everyone else will get the good ships and we'll end up with one made of cabbage crates. Bye, Mum."

Avon grumbled a goodbye as she inspected the flattened remains of her ratty tea, and the boys ran down to the docks.

"What have you brought with you?" Weed said excitedly. "I've got a fishing net and three smooth pebbles, in case we need to haggle for trinkets."

"I'm not sure foreigners deal in smooth pebbles," Mort said. "Who knows what lands afar use as currency, or what we can offer?"

"I'll offer them these if they don't give us what

we want!" Weed held up his two little fists, then quickly lowered them again. "Sorry, Mort. I forgot the Pacifist Promise. Must be nerves."

"I know, Weed. Come on, let's say it now so we don't forget. I've got a feeling that our dedication to being pacifists is going to be challenged on this journey and challenged hard."

Placing their hands on their hearts, the boys closed their eyes and recited the Pacifist Promise in unison:

"I, a member of the Pacifist Society of Brutalia, promise not to hurt anything."

They hugged but were torn apart by a loud *PAAAAAAAAARP* that ripped through the air. It was the incredibly annoying blast of a hundred royal horns.

The Queen was on her way, and they were late.

CHAPTER FOUR
A BOAT CALLED
CᵣABBAGE

"Humans are pretty mean.
We're not mean, are we, Larry?"

"Well... You can be a little shellfish."

"What do you mean?"

"You never shell out for anything."

Most of the fleet were already taken and the people on board were throwing up over the side. This is because Brutalia had no sheltered harbour, only a dark bay of queasy waters, and the ships were tethered between rocks that were spread across the cove like a rash.

rise, dip, lurch, lean, rise, dip, lurch, lean, rise, dip, lurch, lean, rise, dip, lurch, lea

Mort wondered if he had the stomach, eyes and teeth for this. Weed rushed down to the edge of the rickety pier they called 'the docks'. He wanted to catch any giant eels that might bob up to see what all the vomiting was about.

It was unfortunate timing.

At that very moment, the Royal Ship Guard started hurrying people on to the remaining boats before the Queen got her godly knickers in a twist. He towered over Mort. "That ship over there. Go."

"But I'm waiting for my friend."

"You'll be waiting in the dungeons if you don't get a move on!"

Before Mort could shout out to Weed, the guard

kicked his backside towards an unsteady vessel. It was more of a boat than a ship. And more of a rubbish tip than a boat. Its name was scrawled in peeling paint along the prow:

"The *Cabbage*? Is it made from cabbage crates?" Mort asked shakily.

"No, no, no, no," said the guard. "Look, there's an 'r' squished in there. *Crabbage*. It's a regular crabbing boat."

Mort wasn't sure he believed that. But the guard was now prodding him up the ladder with a pointy spear. "Get a move on, boy. Your sailing partner's already on board. Oh, and good luck."

Mort's sailing partner was supposed to be Weed – best friend and part-time pacifist – so he was feeling upset even before he climbed on deck. Then he saw who his new teammate was... It was none other than Punky Mason – a rock-crusher's daughter, and a pacifist's nightmare.

Oh dear.

People avoided rock crushers more than they avoided the plague. Because, while the plague made your insides ooze slowly out of your nose, a rock-crusher squeezed them quite quickly out of your ears, and I know which one I'd go for. The Masons were frankly, truthfully, honestly **TERRIFYING**. They believed affection sapped your strength and that meekness was weakness. Getting close to one almost always meant injury or death.

So is it any wonder that Mort gulped as Punky turned to face him? And what a face... Parts of it were pierced with nails, her mouth was snarling like a wolverine with a nervous twitch, and she had circled her ice-blue eyes with a ring of coal dust. And then there was her voice, hard and rasping like gravel in a blender.

"You gonna say anything or just stand there, looking like a sea cucumber?"

She spat five times in Mort's direction and he looked away – to avoid the spit and because it was a nasty habit. She moved a step closer and he was too scared to speak.

"So you ARE a sea cucumber," she growled. "Great, that's all I need. Someone who'd rather be wobbling around on the floor than hunting for treasure."

She took *another* step closer. *Hang on a minute...*

Mort looked at her.

"Are you playing What's the Time, Mr Wolf?" he asked carefully.

"No!" she spat, but Mort saw a blush of embarrassment on her cheeks. She quickly made up for it by raising a pierced eyebrow and shooting out another sea-based insult. "Oh, so the brainless jellyfish *can* talk. Listen up, I'm serious about getting this Demi-God blessing, so if we fail, I'll kill you. Get it?"

Mort got it and hoped that would be the end of the conversation. But Punky slammed one of her huge fists into the palm of her other hand.

"One wrong move and I'm going to shred you faster than a shark... I'll smash you into smithereens like a sun-dried urchin... I'll..."

Because he couldn't close his ears, Mort closed his eyes and wondered if all her insults were going to involve painful encounters with sea creatures.

"...shove a **stingray up your nose**."

Yep, it did look like all her insults were going to involve painful encounters with sea creatures.

PARP-PA-PA-PAAAAAAARP!

The really annoying royal horns parped again, and
Punky finally shut up because even the toughest girl
on the island didn't want hornets in her pants.

Her Majesty was carried down to the docks,
sitting on a chair on top of a pole. She pulled out her
megaphone and began to speak.

"My loyal subjects!" she shrieked. "It is with
GREAT JOY that I see you depart today. For although
the sea is **vicious** and **cruel**..."

*Her harsh words made Mort think of his dad and
Gosh and Gee out there on the **vicious** and **cruel** sea,
and tears began to brew.*

"...and has claimed the life of nearly everyone who
has **flailed about** in it..."

*Now Mort imagined his dad and Gosh and Gee
flailing about in the freezing chop, and the tears
stormed behind his eyes...*

"...and at least ninety-five per cent of you will be eaten by slimy things that live in it, I know that you have chosen to do this for me, your Queen, your God, your God Queen."

The crowd cheered, and the bounty hunters on the ships waved and grinned as if they were already heroes, but Mort bit his lip. He wasn't doing this for the Queen. He was doing it for his family. Thoughts of them stampeded across his brain like Grot Bears chasing a kitten. If only he'd convinced them to become vegetarian, they wouldn't have been hunting for limpets. If they hadn't been hunting for limpets, they wouldn't have been clinging to the rocks. If they hadn't been clinging to the rocks, the waves wouldn't have plucked them off and tossed them into the thundering waves...

But persuading his family to eat vegetables was harder than persuading Punky Mason not to kill him. And that moment seemed closer than ever because two things had happened during this brief moment of sorry contemplation.

I. Mort had started crying properly. The full-on blub, where tears spurt and your nose wrinkles into an ugly ball with extra big nostril holes to let the snot out.

2. Punky had won What's the Time, Mr Wolf? and was standing right up against him, boring through his eyelids with her frosted laser-beam eyes.

"Are you *crying*?" Punky hissed. "Am I setting out on a dangerous mission with a CRYBABY? You shrimp," she snarled.

"Don't you mean *wimp*?"

"Yeah, I meant to say wimp. You're a wimp. And I'm warning you – if I see one more sign of weakness, you'll be—"

"At the bottom of the sea, being eaten by sea slugs?"

"No—"

"Ripped apart by huge flesh-eating turtles?"

"No, I—"

"Smothered by a giant clam with five faces?"

There was silence. Mort was shocked at the terrible images his sadness had conjured and the

not-caring that came with despairing. Because
he really should be caring about what he said to a
murderous rock-crusher. But this time he'd got away
with it, because Punky Mason had turned a strange
shade of green and was now leaning over the side of
the boat.

In the water below, giant eels waited to see if
she'd throw up.

CHAPTER FIVE
FLOATY BOATY

"I think I've got something in common with that Mort character, Bruce."

"Oh yeah, what's that then?"

"I pass a fish every day."

"It's pacifist, Larry. Pacifist."

The Queen blew a whistle and the ships cast off their ropes, ready to head out into the Salty Sea. But it's never that easy with Brutalians, who will fight at even the most inconvenient times. It doesn't take much to set them off and being splashed a bit by accident will do it.

There was a lot of *being splashed a bit by accident*. Also a lot **not** by accident.

Within seconds of whichever splashing it was, they were leaping from deck to deck, throwing punches, anchors and cuttlefish. And the minutes ticked by.

The Queen, who usually loved a good dust-up, became as irritable as a boil on a bottom and shouted down to her guards, "Fire a warning – come on!"

KA-BOOOM!

Cannonballs sank three ships instantly.

The ready-steady adventurers who weren't deafened or drowning hurried to prepare their vessels before the Queen used her great guns again.

But what happened to the good ship *Crabbage*?

I'm glad you asked that because this story needs a direction, and if it's not the same direction as the *Crabbage* we'll be terribly lost at sea (like a person who doesn't know the third letter of the alphabet).

So, WHAT HAPPENED to the good ship *Crabbage*?

Let's see... Was the good ship *Crabbage* embroiled in a ding-dong? Was it wrecked by Brutalia's quarrelsome fools? Was it spiralling towards the seabed like a drunken mermaid?

No. Thanks to Punky's puking, the *Crabbage* had attracted a huge mass of giant eels. They

writhed under and round the rickety boat, helping
it slide away from the docks and through the rocks
without a scratch. It sped forward on its slippery
conveyor belt, leaving behind the sorry mess at the
ramshackle port. And Weed.

As a widening stretch of sea yawned between the
Crabbage and the land, Mort searched the receding
docks for his friend. There he was, struggling with
what looked like a giant crab.
Mort wanted to turn the boat round, but the
eels kept pushing it forward. He never got to say
goodbye, and who knew if he'd ever see Weed again?
Mort's misery swelled.

"We're off!" Punky said, slapping Mort between
the shoulder blades. "What's the plan? If you haven't
got one, I'm going to kill you."

Plan? Mort panicked. He had a plan, but he
wasn't going to tell her *that* plan. The only other
one that sprang to mind was getting well away from
crazy-face Punky, and as quickly as possible.

"*Well?*" Punky spat. "No plan, no teeth."

Mort wondered why *she* didn't have a plan, but

thought better of asking her when he saw her fists clench. "We're out of the docks first, so we have the advantage. I'll stand at the front of the boat. You stand at the back of the boat. If you see anything, shout."

Mort rushed to the prow and wiped his brow. He didn't know how much more he could take of the scary rock-crusher girl and the sooner they found a trophy, the sooner the *Crabbage* nightmare would be over...

BUT.

(And it was a very big **but**.) The sooner the *Crabbage* nightmare was over, the less time he would have to hunt for Dad, Gosh and Gee.

Memories bobbed up like seagulls in a selfie. He sniffed as he recalled his siblings knocking each other's teeth out adorably. He sobbed as he remembered Dad returning from his day down the drains, grinning through a face full of don't-ask. He wept as he recollected them all round the dinner table, laughing over a meal of rats and rotten potato pie... Maybe they would again.

After half an hour at sea, bored of the endless stretch of miserable grey, Punky became restless. And while Mort was daydreaming and tear-dropping, Punky was playing the creeping-up game again. She made it all the way across the deck without being heard and was now pointing her fingers directly at his peepers. "If I take your eyes out, you won't be able to cry any more."

One look at her face and he knew she meant it. If Mort wanted to keep his eyeballs right where they were, he would need a distraction.

"Trophy!" Mort shouted, pointing at a random spot in the ocean.

"Where? Where? WHERE?" Punky said excitedly. "I can't see anything."

Mort shrugged. "Oh. Must have been a fish. Never mind."

"*Never mind?*" Punky whispered.

"**I MIND!**" she said.

"**I MIND!**" she shouted.

"**I MIND!**" she screamed.

Her voice then fell to a hiss, like a water snake, full of salt and suspissssshion. "I'm wondering if

I should just get rid of you now, you little shrimp."

"*Wimp*. And there *is* treasure!"

"I don't believe you, shrimp."

"It's *wimp*. And there really is treasure. Look, for crying out loud!"

"Crying out loud is for little shrimps."

"For the last time, it's *wimps*. But I'm serious, Punky. **TREASURE AHOY!**"

Punky finally tore her cold stare from Mort's face and pointed it at the horizon. Her mouth fell into a big O and she blinked four times, really quickly.

"All right then," she said. "Let's get the *Crabbage* moving!"

There was just one problem – they didn't how to sail. To make things worse, the eels had slipped away and the *Crabbage* had sunk lower in the waves. Water was leaking through cracks that had been covered up with paper.

"Oh cabbages!" Mort swore.

But, after madly hoisting the sail, they finally caught a strong wind that lifted the boat up and it skidded across the waves towards its goal.

Punky stood at the helm, peering through her fists, which she had curled over each eye to look like binoculars.

"It's gold and silver, I reckon," she said. "Want a look?" She placed her giant fists over Mort's eyes, which was mildly terrifying. But also surprising.

"Your hands are so soft!"

"The rock dust rubs off the dead skin cells, revealing the soft skin underneath. I know, it's not what you'd expect. Now forget about my beautiful hands and tell me what you see out there."

"I don't know but it looks good, Punky. It flickers like gold and glints with the brilliance of twenty saucepans."

CHAPTER SIX
THE INSIDE OF AN URCHIN

"Bored, bored, bored."

"To pass the time, shall we have
a go at some good insults?"

"Okay, I'll start: chips."

"What do you mean, chips?"

"Good in salt."

"Forget it."

It was twenty saucepans.

The golden flicker was merely the flame from a portable stove. Apparently, in the middle of the ocean, floating on an enormous raft, was a fully equipped kitchen.

"Never mind," Mort said again nervously.

"Never mind?

I MIND!

I MIND...!

I MIIIIIIIND!"

Punky screamed so hard that three seagulls fell out of the sky and were scoffed by salty sharks (the Salty Sea's most notorious scavengers), and Mort got a good view of her uvula*.

Dangly bit at the back of the throat. You've got one. Seriously, take a look.

He was surprised it wasn't pierced. She screamed again and he wondered if she'd stepped on a jellyfish. But it wasn't really an OW scream. More of a HOWL scream coming from some place deep down in her soul.

Her voice cracked with emotion. "I MIND! I *miiiiiiiind!*" she spluttered.

There must be a reason she keeps saying that! Mort thought. "Why do you mind so much?"

She stared ahead, eyes watering. Then everything seemed to stop. The sea shushed and the creaking deck hushed. It was so silent you could hear an urchin pop.

Punky wiped her nose along the back of her hand. Then wiped the back of her hand across the front of Mort's top. "You don't know what it's like being me," she said. "Dad says rock crushing is the best job there is. That it's what I was born to do. But I don't know. I think I want more than that..."

After her astonishingly soft hands, Mort thought there couldn't possibly be any more surprises. But he was wrong, and he didn't know what to do. "Oh, Punky, you poor thing."

"Don't give me your pity," she growled.

But Mort was now being controlled by his dominant caring side. He wrapped his arms round her and hugged her tightly, hoping to soothe her.

Before Mort could say, "There, there," he had

been thrown violently across the deck. Below, the salty sharks cackled with expectation.

"I've heard your nickname, *Mort the Meek*. You might be soft, but don't think for one minute I am just because I told you my inner thoughts. I can still rip your head off, you know."

Her vicious side returned with a vengeance, and she glared at Mort while piercing her ear with the spine of a sea urchin. Mort wondered if that was hygienic. He also wondered if they were related – rock crushers and sea urchins. Because now he knew that, under that spiky exterior, Punky had a soft centre, just like urchins. But then she was also a bit like a sea snail because she retreated into her shell when touched. Actually, she was a bit like a clam, the way she opened up and then shut tight again. But maybe she was more like a—

"Dirty sea slug!"

"I wasn't going to say that!" Mort panicked, worried that the conversation in his head had leaked into real life.

"No, I'm calling YOU a dirty sea slug. Turn the *Crabbage* round. We've wasted enough time already talking about feelings and stuff." Punky spat on the deck as if feelings were gross. "And we don't know how much longer this stupid boat will stay afloat."

She was right about that. Leaks had sprung up all over the place and they were now standing knee high in seawater soup. As he hoisted the soggy sail, Mort looked once more at the raft and thought how strange it was – a kitchen floating on a raft in the Salty Sea! Stranger still, a man in a kitchen floating on a raft in the Salty Sea...

Yes, there was a man on board. And, unless Mort was very much mistaken, he was wearing a T shirt that said:

I FIX BOATS WHILE U WAIT

This was serendipity*.

*Serendipity is a bit of good luck

(in this case it's not going dippity into the Salty Sea).

Even Punky agreed that it was a very handy piece of luck and within seconds they were sitting aboard the raft of the wild eyed Tar Jibet, a floating boat repairman who said he could definitely fix your leaks while you waited. Which was very good news as the *Crabbage* was now so low in the water that fish were flopping in and out of it like a saloon bar.

"Looks like an easy enough job," Tar Jibet said, after giving it the once over. "It's so simple, I won't even charge you. But, before I start work, let me get you two settled with some food." He slopped stew, hot from his kitchen, into bowls. "Nothing fancy, but it's good and nourishing."

It did taste good and nourishing, although Mort had to avoid the stringy bits that looked non vegetarian.

"Mr Jibet, have you seen anyone floating by recently? People who might be shipwrecked or lost?" Mort noticed Punky looking at him strangely. "J-j-just making f-friendly conversation," he mumbled. "It's the sort of thing you ask people at sea, isn't it?"

"Yes." Tar nodded.

"Yes, you've seen people floating by?" Mort asked hopefully.

"Yes, it's the sort of thing you ask people at sea. But no, I haven't seen people floating by. Before you arrived, I'd not seen a soul for weeks. Say, what brings you two out on the Salty Sea?"

"Treasure, of course," Punky said, still moody about the saucepans. She picked bits of crab shell from her teeth and flicked them at the salty sharks who picked them out of their teeth and spat them right back.

"Oh, so no doubt you were attracted by my shiny pans. I hope you haven't gone too far off course, chasing my kitchen. It wouldn't be the first time..."

"Tell us where to find treasure or I'll throw your pots into the sea," Punky said, narrowing her eyes.

"It wouldn't be the first time," he chuckled again.

"I'll toss you to the sharks," she threatened.

"Wouldn't be the first time." Tar raised his left leg, revealing a foot made out of a wooden crate.

"I'll gut you like a fish."

"Calm down, Little Miss Angry," he laughed, running his fingers through his wispy eyebrows.

"She says that to everyone," Mort said nervously. "It's a term of affection in Brutalia. We always say things like, 'I think you're nice – *so I'll gut you like a fish.*'"

What Punky didn't seem to have realized was that they were out at sea with a broken boat, surrounded by sharks. They should probably keep on Tar Jibet's good side, especially as he had so selflessly offered to mend the *Crabbage* for free.

"No offence taken," he said, eyes twinkling. "Tell me – what good is treasure to Brutalia? I hear pebbles are the only currency on that rock of despair."

"The Queen has discovered that she's descended from a god and we're on a mission to find her the finest trophies and trinkets."

"A god, you say? Well now, normal treasure won't do for a god. Gold, silver, jewels ... that's for pirates. What you need is—"

Tar jumped up and rattled his pans.

DERR-DUM-DERR-DUM-DERR-DUM-DERR-DUM

"Saucepans?" Mort and Punky asked at once.

"No, not saucepans. I just needed a dramatic tune that suggests monsters are close by. Gods love that stuff – monsters and beasts. And there's nothing they love more than a trophy from a monster fight. And, as it happens, over there I have something that would suck your socks off."

"What is it?" Mort asked.

The man tapped his nose and tiptoed over to a pile of bits and pieces on the other side of the raft, covered with a sheet of tarpaulin.

Punky nudged Mort. *"This is stupid,"* she whispered angrily. *"He looks like a madman and talks like a madman. He's been at sea on his own too long. He'll probably come back with a rubber duck or an inflatable ring. Let's go."*

"No, we should give him the benefit of the—"

Mort swallowed his last unspoken words as Tar Jibet, hair waving wildly in the breeze, made his way back across the rippling raft, rolling an ENORMOUS inflatable ring.

"It's not what it looks like," Tar chortled, but Punky was already on her feet, reaching for a shiny saucepan.

CHAPTER SEVEN
THE
SWISH-SWASH

"I met an octopus once. He was all right, nice fellow."

"All those dangly bits, no thank you very much.
I'd rather hang out with a shark."

"Why on earth would you rather hang out with a shark?"

"Because they're armless."

Punky and Mort lay still, staring up at the seagulls. No, they weren't on a beach holiday – that's a different story called *Mort and Punky's Beach Holiday*, which hasn't happened yet. This is a cold, hard sea story. But what had just happened?

A giant wave had come out of nowhere and put them flat on their backs, that's what.

"Did you enjoy my swish-swash?" Tar chuckled, pointing to a wooden handle. "It pulls a rudder under the middle of the raft which creates a wave that destabilizes anything standing on top. It's for self-defence."

They tried to get to their feet, but he pulled the swish-swash again, creating another wave. And then another. And another. And the raft rippled over and over again like a never-ending wave. *Maybe Tar Jibet is mad,* thought Mort.

Eventually, Tar stopped and let the seasick Brutalian children get upright again.

"No doubt you two think I'm mad. But I do not appreciate being attacked with one of my own trusty saucepans."

"We're sorry. *Aren't we, Punky*," Mort said firmly.

Punky's jaw remained fixed, like chiselled stone.

Tar Jibet grinned. "No harm done. You're only kids. And kids love stories, so let me tell you one. The story is honestly true and it's about how I came to be in possession of *this*."

He tapped the enormous inflatable ring. But we've already said this isn't a beach story... What was he talking about?

"Two weeks ago a monster came to see me. It wrapped itself round my raft. Took me for a ride to the Exotics, then to the Tropics, then to the Marshlands, then to the Harshlands, and then back round the Salty Sea three times before letting me go. And, when it did, its sucker got caught in my swish-swash and popped right off..."

Mort's eyes grew as big as beachballs (but this still isn't a beach story). "Wait, are you saying that's a sucker?" he gasped. "If that's a *sucker*, it must have come from a *giant* octopus."

"Bigger than that!" Tar winked.

"A colossal-giant octopus?" Punky tried.

"Bigger than that."

"A gargantuan-leviathan-giant-octopus-like behemoth?" Mort suggested.

"Bigger than that."

"Get on with it!" Punky screamed.

"My little Brutalian friends..." Tar's voice adopted an air of mystery, and his face adopted some eyebrow-waggling which ruffled his hair. "It was none other than..."

The hanging saucepans rattled in the wind,

DEN-DEN-DEEEEEEEEEEEEEER

"The Belgo!"

He said it in a whisper, and the air was full of suspense.

DE-CLANG-DE-WHALLOP -DI-BISH-BOSH-DUM

The saucepans didn't do such a good job that time,

but it didn't matter because no tune could be dramatic enough for what Tar Jibet had just uttered. Mort's jaw dropped, one of Punky's piercings pinged out and goosebumps prickled up and down their arms.

So, you ask, what on earth was the Belgo?

(More dramatic, please!)

WHAT ON EARTH WAS
THE BELGO?

(Much better.)

Everyone in the Salty Sea knows exactly what the Belgo is, so this is for your benefit. Yes, YOU! Are you sitting uncomfortably? Good, now pay attention.

A Short Lesson About the Belgo

The Belgo was like an octopus, but the size of the Eiffel Tower. It had five arms less than a regular octopus (which is THREE if you don't like doing maths). They were longer than the distance between here and there, as thick as houses and lined with suckers that could each comfortably encompass the entire face of an African elephant. Two eyes rolled like giant gobstoppers in its domed head, its body was an orange torpedo and its breath was... Actually, its breath was fine.

The Belgo hadn't been seen for so many years it had become a myth. But long ago it wasn't just a legend, so the story goes. The story even goes on to say that there was once a permanent lookout on Brutalia's highest cliff and, if the Belgo was spotted, a bell would be clanged over and over. Then chatter would race through the town like rabbits:

"I think I just heard the bell go!"
"Did you hear the bell go?"
"Did the bell go?"

Or just

"Bell go!"

But why it was called the Belgo, nobody knows.

Whatever the origin, that name was easier to say than the Latin one, which is:

Aliquam triduo polypus ingens armis

But let's get back to Tar Jibet's raft, where the inflatable ring has suddenly become the most excellent trophy.

"Please, Mr Jibet, this is the perfect curiosity to present to our Queen. Is there anything we can give you in return for the Belgo sucker?" Mort pleaded.

"Well, I'm a humble and honest man and I never like to take anything for myself," Tar said. "Tell you what, let me fix the *Crabbage* for you before it sinks and then we can talk about the details."

And so Tar Jibet set to work.

First, he moved his stove and pans aboard the rickety boat – in order to boil tar, he said. He then moved the rest of his kitchen things aboard the boat – in order to make tea and keep warm while he worked, he said. He then moved all his other belongings on board the *Crabbage* – to test how much weight the boat could take, he said.

And then he set sail.

And suddenly all those things **he had said** that sounded too good to be true sounded a bit like lies.

"Where are you going?" Mort yelled. "You're stealing our boat!"

Tar Jibet, whose eyes twinkled with deception, leaned over the side and yelled back, "I'm bored with rafting. I want the ups and downs of sailing, the bucking and the heave-ho, the pitching from side to side. It's the closest thing I'll ever get to being a Rock 'n' Roll Tar."

BOOM-TISH went his saucepans.

"But what about us? What are we supposed to do?"

"You can have the *Big Susan* – my raft. And that stupid inflatable ring I found drifting out at sea."

"You told us it was a Belgo sucker."

"I told you a lot of things. And the Belgo is a myth. Looks like YOU'RE the suckers now!" he hooted. And then he was gone.

Mort felt like crying. It had been his idea, all of it. He'd trusted the words on a T-shirt. He'd believed that when a man seemed kind and said he was honest he meant it. And now they were doomed.

Punky was so furious she'd shaken herself rigid. And Mort was worried that the slightest thing might set her off. Out here, in the middle of the Salty Sea on a flat raft called the *Big Susan*, there was nowhere to hide. But eventually something had to be said.

"Punky, I—"

"ARGHGHRGHGHGHGHG!"

Punky shook herself free of her furious statue and ran from one side of the *Big Susan* to the other, kicking the air, punching the sky and yelling stuff that we really, really can't repeat.

"Punky!" Mort tried again, but to no avail.

The rock-crusher looked like she could break
mountains. Or him. And, uh-oh, she had begun
running towards him – fast, graceful and muscular,
like a killer ballerina doing the hundred-metre sprint
on sports day – with a ferocity in her eyes that could
blast crystals to smithereens. To Mort's horror, she
stopped, pulled out a nail from her eyebrow, pointed it
in his direction and charged.

He couldn't fight back – he was a pacifist – so he
was done for. He closed his eyes and prepared to be

pierced in some place horrible... Any moment now...
Any moment... But Mort felt a whoosh of air as
Punky ran past him and turned to see her pushing the
nail deep into the inflatable ring.

~~POP~~

~~PFFFT~~

~~BANG~~

None of those sounds happened. Punky pulled
out the nail and stabbed it again. But the inflatable
ring didn't pop. Again and again, the nail sank into
the rubbery texture and did nothing more than
release a faintly fishy smell. All she wanted was a
satisfying explosion... Everything was going wrong.

"Oh my goodness. It IS a sucker," Mort said.
"And it's the sucker of something really big!"

Punky wiped a coal-stained tear of frustration
from her cheek and stepped forward. "I don't believe
in the Belgo. Do you?"

"I don't know. Even if it's just from the biggest octopus in the sea, it's enough to impress. It's still a monster of sorts. That dishonest fool was telling the truth and he didn't even know it! Punky, we've got our trophy."

Punky tossed the nail into the sea (where it pierced the eyebrow of a passing salty shark) and sank to her knees. She wrapped her arms round the sucker and smiled. "Let's go home," she said in a small, exhausted voice.

Mort nodded encouragingly, but inside his heart broke.

Searching for his dad and Gosh and Gee had been *his* reason for embarking on this mad trip. He didn't care about trophies and god status and character-building experiences. All he'd ever cared about was bringing his family home safe...

Mort stared around him desperately, hoping the writer might have thrown in a last-minute lifeline. Maybe an SOS in the distance – perhaps the grubby pants of a small kid called Gosh or Gee waved on a stick to grab the attention of anyone passing by... But no.

Mort looked over at Punky and thought of that soft centre beneath the spikiness – all the hurt and pain of being a loveless rock-crusher. Becoming a Demi-God meant *everything* to her. And sometimes... Well, sometimes you just had to help whoever needed to be helped right there and then.

So they sailed home and that was that.

YEAH, RIGHT! We're not even halfway through the story, and if you think Mort's going to give up on his family that easily then you don't know Mort. Keep going and you soon will...

CHAPTER EIGHT
SO LONG, SUCKERS

"There's this bloke up there on the dock –
says he wants us to star in a show!"

"Where?"

"On land. This is it, Larry! This is the big time.
We're going to be entertainers!"

"We're going to be in containers? No, Bruce, no!"

"I think you've got
seaweed in your
earhole, Larry."

Mort and Punky quickly discovered why the dishonest Tar Jibet was so eager to abandon his raft and snaffle the *Crabbage*. The *Big Susan* had no functioning wheel, oars or sails. To get moving, they used the only thing left unbroken – the swish-swash. He and Punky took turns yanking the handle over and over, flapping the *Big Susan* like a bored jellyfish all the way home to Brutalia. It was a yawningly long period of discomfort and seasickness.

For Mort and Punky – tossed by the turbulent sea and slapped in the face by flying seaweed, fish and various wet and wobbly things – the days felt long and their skin felt cold. They were forced to huddle together for warmth. Punky reminded Mort every hour – with a stony glare and a raised fist – that this was only for survival and he wasn't to go thinking she liked him or anything. But, when she let down her guard, they talked and played. They swapped terrible jokes to pass the time; Punky told stories of funny-shaped rocks and her dreams of a better-shaped life; and Mort talked about pacifism and his dreams of spreading kindness.

Then what happened? I'll tell you what happened: whether they admitted it or not, Mort and Punky became friends.

What else happened? I'll tell you what else happened: Punky asked Mort to give her a tattoo as a reminder of their adventure (which he didn't do because he hadn't any ink or a good tattoo design).

Did anything *else* happen? Yes, I'll tell you what else happened: during those long days and nights of drifting and flopping, when Punky was sleeping, Mort frantically searched the miserable grey sea for any sign of Dad and Gosh and Gee. But there was nothing. Not a scrap of clothing. Not even a whiff. No blast of the twins' ripe body odour on the wind or a sickly tendril of his father's favourite scent, **Eau de Errr de Plumber** (which Olfa Smelch had made specially for him by adding the words 'de Plumber' and charging him an extra pebble). They were gone, gone, gone.

GONE. Such an empty and forlorn word, Mort thought sadly.

After many more hours and many more forlorn words...

"We're finally here!" declared Mort as the *Big Susan* slumped against the rocks by the docks of Brutalia. The place was totally empty apart from a single guard, who appeared to be training a row of lobsters to dance.

"You want fame? Well, fame costs, and right here is where you start paying in sweat. One, two, one, two, turn round and kick. Kick!"

"Ahoy there!" Mort rasped through his salt-coated throat, but the sound spluttered no further than a few sea slugs.

"Not backwards and forwards! Side to side, I said. Argh! I should have used crabs!"

"Oi!" Punky shouted, using all her breath. And a well-aimed urchin.

The guard told his lobsters to take five minutes' rest. As they scuttled to the side of the docks, he put his hands on his hips and narrowed his eyes. "Well, well. I wasn't expecting to see *you* back," he said.

Punky punched the air. "We're first, right? I knew we would be."

The guard stifled a giggle. "Sorry, rock-crusher. You're the last ones back. In fact, we thought you were dead you've been gone so long. I'm only down here because it's a quiet place to train the lobsters."

He tossed over a rope and heaved the *Big Susan* closer to land, before securing the raft between the rocks. Mort and Punky leaped on to solid ground, careful not to step on any dancers.

"Why are you training lobsters to dance?" Mort asked.

"It's for the Grand God Feast. I'm in charge of the crustacean show. And it's not just any dance – it's the salsa."

"Right... And what is a Grand God Feast?"

"Oh, you have missed a lot. The Queen's invited suitors to a big party. She's choosing a new King. There'll be singing and dancing and flirting. And, for the grand finale, she'll crown the Demi-Gods. Rumour has it she's already chosen the winner – some lone bounty hunter called Lucky Golightly. He stumbled on a cave of ancient statues just round the bay. What have you got there – an inflatable ring?"

Punky's face turned stony as the Demi-God crown slipped from her grasp, and she visualized crushing this Lucky Golightly to a pulp.

"It's the sucker of a sea monster," Mort said. "It might even be from the Belgo."

The guard jumped backwards like an electrocuted starfish. And the lobsters jumped backwards like electrocuted lobsters.

"Not ... the BELGO?"

Somewhere out at sea twenty saucepans rattled in the wind...

DEN-DEN-DEEERRRRRRRRR

Mort, Punky, the guard and the lobsters waited until the sound dissolved in the fizzing spray, to get the full dramatic effect. Then the guard whispered something to his snappy dancers, and they slipped back over the rocks into the wash.

"Don't forget to practise!" he yelled before turning back to Mort and Punky. "Tell you what, kids – it might not be Lucky's lucky day after all. I'll take you to the palace."

The Queen narrowed her eyes at the sight of Mort. Had they met before? Oh yes, they most certainly had (you'll have to read the first book to find out why, because this story's absolutely chocka). But, when the guard announced the details of the trophy, her eyes quickly un-narrowed and popped open with glee. Awkwardness at seeing Mort vanished as fast as a golden cockle in a pirate's pie. She rubbed her hands with glee.

"Oh, this is good, this is good," she oozed, her

words slippery with greed. "I will claim that a Brutalian under my rule did battle the Belgo—"

"*Probably* the Belgo," Mort said, wanting to be totally honest. "We can't be sure."

"Either way, this monstrous trophy will act as a reminder that nobody can outdo the God Queen."

Lots of courtiers clapped and cheered and bowed and curtseyed, which is called sucking up. (This story is riddled with suckers, I tell you.)

"I think your Demi-God blessing is in the bag," whispered the guard, who couldn't stand Lucky Golightly after he'd said the lobsters danced like floundering amateurs. Punky flushed with joy.
It looked as if her wish would come true.

But at that moment a flustered fisherman skidded into the palace hall with a large cloth sail rolled under his arm.

"What is going on?" the Queen demanded.

The fisherman opened his mouth, but couldn't speak – he looked as if he was mute with shock.
He laid out his sail in the centre of the marble floor and stood back. Marked upon it was a greasy circle,

as large as the entire face of an African elephant. The Queen, being in a good mood, did not send him off to the dungeons for the crime of bursting into the Royal Palace. Instead she raised herself to a standing position upon the backs of two children and made them shuffle on hands and knees round the mysterious mark.

"Let me guess, it's a flag.

No – a map of a round country.

No – a portal to another dimension.

No – a strange fortune-telling symbol.

No – a fun game.

No – a sumo-fighting ring.

No – a—"

She shot everyone a glare. "For Brutalia's sake, will someone just tell me what it is before I run out of space?"

"Your M-Majesty, it's, it's, it's..."

While the nervous fisherman stumbled over his words, realization hit Mort like a well-aimed cuttlefish between the eyes. He rolled the sucker across the sail and lowered it over the ring-mark. It fitted perfectly.

"The mark was made by a sucker, just like this one," Mort said.

The fisherman nodded and pointed and panted and finally got the rest of his words out. "It's the B-B-Belgo. It's back. And it's right here in Brutalian waters. Saw it with my own eyes – wobbly and orange with three giant arms. No mistaking it. If anyone has gone missing in the last few weeks, I'll bet my boatee* that they're now in the guts of the Belgo. Or worse."

*A long wispy beard that trendy fishermen grow.

"What could be WORSE?" the Queen spat, and no one dared tell her how the digestive system works. She shuffled back to her throne, but to everyone's surprise her face lit up. "This has all turned out rather wonderfully. Not only have these trophy hunters brought me the sucker of the most fearsome beast ever known, we now have an actual witness. Proof it exists! Because to be honest, without proof, it just looks like an inflatable ring, doesn't it?"

Everyone agreed it did a bit.

"Excellent. The feast is in a week's time, and then I shall be able to pick the finest new King. And you two," she said, pointing a finger at Mort and Punky, "will be my chosen Demi-Gods."

Punky punched the air and shouted,

"Demi-God, Yeah!"

She turned to high-five her companion. But Mort was as still and silent as a statue, his mind chewing through the fisherman's words again and again.

If anyone has gone missing in the last few weeks ... they're now in the guts of the Belgo.

"Mort?" Punky pinched him but he didn't flinch.

Something strange was happening to him.

His thoughts were twisted, his face was twisted, his guts were twisted, but his tongue wasn't twisted because the sentence that came out was very clear indeed. It emerged surely and viciously, like words going to war.

"I am going to kill the Belgo."

And a bitter smoke swirled round his heart like the dark breath of a demon.

It was a moment that felt significant, and nobody said a word. There was nothing but the scrunch of the Queen's fake eyelashes (made from tarantula legs) as she widened her eyes. So wide, it looked like her eyeballs might fly out.

Then they narrowed suddenly. Properly evil. "Oh yes," she said in vicious whisper. "Imagine that. Imagine the Belgo *here*, sacrificed at the Grand God Feast by my own hand. What a great display of power that would be. Yes, yes, yes. Bring the Belgo to me alive. And THEN you may have your prize."

Punky's air-punching fist dropped like lead to her side. "You mean we're not going to be Demi-Gods unless we go back out to sea and capture that octopus thing?"

"That's right."

"But we might die."

"That's right."

"But that's so unfair."

"That's right."

"But this sucks!"

"That's right. Now GO!"

Punky turned slowly to look at Mort, her piercings rattling as fury rumbled through every part of her body.

"Mort Canal, you stupid, horrible, filthy little—"

PAAAAAAAAAAAAAAAAAAA AAAAAAAAAAAAAAAARP went the horns. And it was decided.

CHAPTER NINE
UNROLL THE SCROLL

"The big night is drawing near, Larry.
Everyone will be looking at us!"

"But I'm covered in barnacles, Bruce."

"Hmm... There's only one thing for it."

"The place where shellfish
go to get groomed?"

"That's right. Let's go
to the Crust Station!"

"If anyone has gone missing in the last few weeks ... they're now in the guts of the Belgo."

As the fisherman's words turned over and over in his head, Mort marched down the smoky side streets and belchy backstreets of Brutalia. He was Mort on a mission and nothing was going to stop him. Not even things that would usually stop a sweet-natured pacifist, like a little rat holding up a poorly foot for help. He wasn't even delayed by the group of kids who offered him free bruises. Mort strode right through them, hardly feeling the kicks to his shins.

Inside him, the bitter smoke thickened, like the dark breath of a couple more demons.

Nothing could hurt him. Not nasty little kids and not Punky's insult, which had bounced off him like a ripe raven. He was invincible. He was angry.

ABSOLUTELY FUROIUS in fact.

The Belgo had eaten his dad. It had eaten Gosh and Gee.

They were now in its guts (or worse, if you consider the digestive system) and Mort wanted revenge. It spewed and bubbled inside him like a frogspawn smoothie.

But then a sweet voice cut through the darkness. "Mort the Meek! Mort the Meek!"

That gentle nickname, spoken by his best friend and part-time pacifist, Weed, soothed him only for a second before the smoke closed in once again, cloudy and cruel. Mort snarled, "Get lost, I'm in a hurry."

"But it's me – Weed! Mort, you're alive! You're alive! You've been gone so long, I made a dough doll and called it Mort and recited the Pacifist Promise with it every day. Just so I didn't go crazy and punch someone to let off steam. Oh happy days, you're alive! And you must have been worrying about me too, because that's the kind of kind person you are. Aren't you glad I'm alive too, Mort?"

"Oh yeah, you're not dead." Mort looked straight ahead.

"Do you want to know what happened? I missed the launch of the boats. I was attacked by a giant beast of a crab down at the docks. Had me by the neck, it did. I thought I'd be pincered to death and never see you again. But I fought it off, Mort. Fought it with my own bare hands. Aren't you proud?"

"Whatever, Weed. I'm busy."

"You're acting so out of character!" Weed sobbed, but Mort didn't care because he was acting so out of character.

To be sure, let's check our character notes:

NAME: Mort Canal, son of plumbers Avon and Kennet Canal. Older sibling to Gosh and Gee.

CHARACTERISTICS: nice, peaceful, kind, thoughtful, sweet, non-violent, considerate, gentle, selfless, pacifist, non-spitty (unlike a common troll).

Oh yes, he was acting out of character all right. He was barely recognizable as he gobbed like a common troll and shoved Weed aside. But Weed wasn't about to give up. Not without first trying his beautiful-chocolatey-eyes trick. Mort always gave in to his beautiful chocolatey eyes.

Weed ran in front of his friend, forcing him to stop, and then widened his beautiful chocolatey eyes until they were enormous and enchanting like a cartoon woodland creature... But the smoke was thick, Mort's heart was hardening and he looked away. He broke into a run and left Weed wondering what had made him so cross. Was it talking about the crab fight? After all, as a half-member of the Pacifist Society of Brutalia, he shouldn't be fighting anything, not even a giant crab. Mort was never going to upgrade him to a full member at this rate. Weed punched himself in the face for being so stupid and went home.

Mort sped past the grungy guts of the island, past its putrid petticoats, and didn't stop until he was on the 'orrible outskirts of Brutalia, standing in front of the home of Scribe Pockle. The door swung open before Mort could knock.

"Ah, Mort Canal, I've been expecting you," said the old man.

"Have you? Why?"

"Because it saves time," said Scribe Pockle. "Come in, come in. I have the documents you require laid out on the table."

"Documents that might show me how to find the Belgo?"

"The very ones. Come in – quickly now."

On the table a scroll had been unrolled, fixed in place by two stale loaves of bread and hastily covered in used tea bags to make it look old and interesting. Scribe Pockle pushed the tea bags aside so Mort could see the title.

Confronting Beadly Deasts

"Beadly deasts?"

"*Deadly beasts.* It's old spelling," said Scribe. "**B**s and **D**s were interchangeable in the olden days.

Here, this is the dit you neeb."

"Do you mean the *bit you need*?"

"Yes, I do. Now hurry. There isn't much time."

Mort followed Scribe's bony finger as it moved across the parchment, looking for the right paragraph to point at. There. A block of dense, shaky script. Mort scrunched up his eyes and peered closely.

How to finb a Delgo
The Delgo must de wooeb with a meloby.

"*Finb a Delgo?*"

"Find a Belgo," Pockle corrected.

"*The Delgo must de wooeb?*"

"The Belgo must be wooed," Pockle translated.

"*With a meloby?*" Mort said.

"Melody," Scribe groaned through gritted teeth. "Remember the **B**s and **D**s – come on, Mort! But these are the words that will help you, boy, for they come from none other than Singrum Kelp."

Mort gasped. *Singrum Kelp!*

Time for a Quick Lesson
in Brutalian Folklore

Singrum Kelp was the best fisherman the world had ever known, stunning fish of all sizes with his rugged handsomeness and catching them deftly between his toes. He was astoundingly gorgeous. When he left to go fishing, people flocked to the docks to bid him farewell. He departed with a little wink and returned with bags of little winkles (snail-like creatures that, when pickled in potato vinegar, were considered a delicacy – if you liked that sort of thing).

His pockets were full of pearls that oysters had thrown at him in adoration, he wore seaweed necklaces woven by manatees, and there was always an amorous squid or two clinging to his shins. Every creature of land and sea loved him. Even the Queen at that time found herself seduced by his marine-blue eyes and the dozen oysters he brought her every morning, plucked from where he kept them in his boatee. His facial hair was silky and conditioned, his eyebrows told stories, and his voice was like a choir.

His lilting sea shanties made the island of Brutalia buzz with deep and soulful vibrations. Indeed, Singrum Kelp was an extraordinary specimen.

Until he met the Belgo.

After that, he looked a bit like an overcooked frankfurter.

You see, during the wrangle with the beast, he lost an arm, a leg and his luscious boatee. His skin was flayed red raw and his voice turned bitter. He no longer had fishing skills and flabbergasting beauty. And he no longer had the Queen's adoration. She dumped him for a nobleman called Sir Looch of Pluffet.

And now you know the story of Singrum – the only man to face the beast and live to tell the tale. Mort eagerly read what the legendary fisherman had written.

It was the song that did it. My haunting shanty – a song straight from my heart – drew the Belgo to me and it did float, stunned in the water, as I sang. When I finished, so angry was it that the music had gone, it wrapped an arm round my throat. Its terrible eyes turned black with hatred and it squeezed me with the power of a million men. Its suckers could pull the skin from your bones and the hair from your chin. And that is the price I paid for singing a song from my heart. And now I have no songs left, for my heart is broken. I am half the man I was, but I am not half the legend. I am nothing at all. A whole is worth more than two halves. An outrageously stunning man cannot be half outrageously stunning. And because of this terrible equation I have lost my love, the Queen...

It got a bit self-pitying after that so Scribe Pockle lifted the loaves of bread and the scroll sprang back into a tight tube. "There you go. All done?"

"Wait. So, in order to capture the Belgo, I need a song?"

"Looks like it. Now run, quickly. Bye!"

Scribe Pockle was in a hurry because his friends were due any minute for a bottle of mead and an illegal game of Rock, Paper, Scissors. But, in his hot rage, Mort didn't notice the rush.

Smoke choked his heart like the breath of a barbecued demon. And it formed the word

REVENGE.

He found Punky down at the rubble site, slamming her fists into boulders. She had three more piercings and a face like thunder. When she saw Mort, it turned into a face like thunder if thunder was squashed between two panes of glass and heated to ninety degrees.

"What are you doing here?" she said, spitting a gob of brick dust at Mort's feet.

Mort didn't even mind because, in case you hadn't realized, he had **Turned Bad**. "We're setting sail. We're catching the Belgo. Tonight."

"Why would I go?" Punky sneered. "You make a mess of everything you do. You'll probably get us killed."

But Mort needed her help. He couldn't catch the beast on his own. He searched for something to convince her. And the words of Singrum's scroll played at the edges of his mind. *Something about being two halves.*

"You'll never persuade me to do anything with you ever again, you snivelling little clam-bladder," she continued.

Two halves... A whole is worth more than two halves!

"Listen, Punky. If we do this, we will be blessed as Demi-Gods. And I will give MY blessing to YOU. Then you will have **two** Demi-God blessings."

"What would I do with an extra one?" Punky shouted. "Eat it? Throw it in the bin?"

"No, you're not thinking clearly," Mort said. "Do the maths. If Thy has one Demi-God and George gives her another Demi-God, how many Demi-Gods does Thy have?"

"I dunno."

"OK, if Sally McRoot is making soup and adds half a teaspoon of salt. And then adds another half a teaspoon of salt..."

"She'll have added a whole teaspoon of salt."

"That's right. So if I add my Demi-God blessing to yours...?"

"I'll be a WHOLE GOD!"

CHAPTER TEN
SO, LONG SUCKERS

"Did you hear about the Belgo?"

"Yeah, it's a kraken story."

"It's not a story. It's real."

"It's a really kraken story, then."

For the second time, Punky and Mort found themselves at sea. But this time they were not flopping around on the *Big Susan* but sailing with tremendous ease on the Queen's *Golden Behind*. Before you ask, the *Golden Behind* was her very own ship and a little more impressive than the *Crabbage*.

"What do we do now?" Punky asked. "How do we find the Belgo?"

"The scroll said that singing attracts the beast and..." Mort tailed off as he imagined Gosh and Gee singing a cheery round of 'Brutalia's Burning' – the Belgo edging closer with every note... Anger billowed through him. The darkness got thicker and chokier and smokier.

"We are going to sing it to its death." Mort let rip an evil laugh that was extremely out of character.

Mwa-ha-ha-ha-ha-haaaaa!

Even Punky was startled. "You're acting a bit weird. But you can act however you want, just as long as I get the full God blessing. What shall we sing?"

"Try anything."

"I know, how about my family anthem, 'I Just Want To'?" Punky said, breaking into song with a voice that sounded like chainsaws squabbling in a bathtub.

I just want to break rocks, baby.
Smash big blocks, baby.
I'll grind you into dust, maybe
If you don't let me break rocks, baby.
Smash big blocks, baby.
I'll grind you into dust, maybe
If you don't let me break rocks, baby.
Smash big—"

"STOP!" Mort shouted, holding his ears. "It's terrible."

"You sing something then," she said sulkily.

Mort belted out a couple of Brutalian nursery rhymes – 'Hey Widdle Piddle' and 'If You're Unhappy and You Know it, Smash Some Pans' – which attracted several nursery sharks and a couple of whipper-snappers. But not the Belgo. The Salty

Sea thundered on as usual, with no variation in the grey and the monotonous kick of its choppy waves. Mort cried tears of frustration, but he kept singing, determined, searching for a sign of the monster. Until... There, on a distant swell, something appeared. Wreckage. People waving flags that looked like pants on sticks. A voice reached his ears in windy bites.

"Hello! ... Save us ... Help ... or you'll regret it later."

Mort was a pacifist who wanted to prevent harm coming to any living thing. At least that's what he *WAS*. But now he was unrecognizable. And he was hunting for a beast, not humans. He didn't have time for pesky, time-consuming sea rescues, only **revenge**. So the *Golden Behind* sailed on, and Mort stood at the prow of the ship like an angry figurehead. Fixed and furious. Unmoved and unfeeling. Until he was painfully distracted by a well-aimed sea urchin.

"Mort, come here!"

Punky pointed to a spot just below the horizon where a bulge bulged in the water. It was the same size as a really big whale, and as orange as an ice lolly. A ribbon of black ink shot into the air, painting the day to look like night. And the enormity of what was ahead took Mort and Punky by the throat and shook them up, making them drop most of their words.

"Do you think it's...?"

"Yes, I think it's..."

"You mean, it's..."

"Yes. It's..."

Cue saucepans... Where are the saucepans? There are twenty of them out there, for heaven's sake. Oh, never mind.

It's ... THE BELGO!

They cheered loudly but only to hide their nerves. After all, they were just two small children and, alongside this landmark-sized sea beast, they were like prawns waiting to be plucked from a buffet. Only these prawns were going to make the first move.

"This is it, Punky," Mort said, furrowing his brow in concentration. "I'll sing and you get the wire ready. As soon as it's stunned, leap in and bind the arms."

Mort began to sing 'Happy Burpday' – a traditional

tune at one of Brutalia's cabbage festivals – but the
Belgo didn't come closer. In fact, it seemed to be
heading in the opposite direction.

"Wait!" Mort yelled. **"Waaaaaiiiiiiiit!"**

"Ha ha, maybe it didn't like your voice either,"
Punky teased. "Maybe it thinks you sound like a
whelk with a mouthful of gravel."

It's true. Mort's voice, which was usually melodic,
was sour (a side effect of having your lungs filled with
the putrid breath of demons). But there was something
else. Something he was forgetting... He paced the
deck, his mind going over the words of Singrum Kelp.

My haunting shanty – a song straight from my heart

"It's not our voices, it's the song! It wants
something meaningful. A heart song."

"My heart doesn't have a song," Punky said.
"What's in yours?"

Mort closed his eyes and allowed his heart
to open, pouring his smouldering torment into
a surprisingly good tune.

"You horrible beast, can't you see?
You've eaten my precious family.
I hate you with every part of me.
Belgo, I will be the end of thee."

There was an intense bubbling like a giant's jacuzzi, and the bulge edged closer.

"It's working, it's working! Sing some more!"

The Belgo moved towards the *Golden Behind*, arms trailing like a massive dangly torpedo, and Mort raised his voice and revealed even more of his troubled dark heart in a bitter, sad song...

"You horrible beast, can't you see?
You've taken away my Gosh and Gee.
Come closer and fish food you will be,
I'll chop you into calamari..."

"Mort. That's way too aggressive! You're acting so out of character."

Punky was right. The Belgo (not thrilled at the idea of being chopped into calamari) put on its brakes.

It raised its head above the water. It was huge, it was beastly and it was not happy. And its eyes – the size and colour of coalpits – searched the *Golden Behind* for the owner of the vicious song. It raised two of its arms above the water – terrifyingly huge slithering ropes pocked with sucker cups – and as one wrapped itself round the ship, the other began plucking salty sharks out of the sea and throwing them on to the deck.

"Now look what you've done, Mort!" said Punky, dodging a toothy shark.

"I'd like to see *you* try!" Mort yelled, hurdling another. "Your voice could make a city crumble. Not to mention your face!"

Usually, Punky would have inserted sharp stones into painful places after such a horrible comment, but instead she stormed to the other side of the boat. Her chest felt tight and her heart beat fast. And her feelings were ... hurt. She felt like a shrimp. Everything had been so difficult. Now Mort the Meek – the one person she was sure wouldn't be mean – had started being a horrible old urchin. She looked out to sea and a song began to play on her lips.

"A lowly rock-crusher girl am I.
I want so much more from life – big sigh!
I wish my surprisingly smooth, soft hands
Could do something else in these troubled lands."

Mort was going to shout something about her voice sounding like cats fighting on a hot tin roof, but the Belgo had stopped throwing sharks and was rocking the ship from side to side. Mort was terrified and thrilled all at once. He opened a hatch in the ship's side and kicked a shark overboard.

"Keep singing!" he shouted, shaking a keen shark from his ankle. "Sing, Punky!"

"Are you being sarcastic?" she shouted back. "It's not nice."

"It's not nice to throw urchins, but you still do it."

"It's just what's expected of me, because I'm a lowly rock-crusher."

"Sing about it!" Mort yelled. "Sing about your pain and unfulfilled dreams NOW!"

It was time. Mort gulped like a goldfish out of water – the Belgo could swallow the ship whole if it wanted! But with its arms safely beneath the surface, it swam alongside, staring up with giant orb eyes like a love-struck bath toy. Punky's vocals might have sounded like electric drills caught in a lawnmower, but the Belgo was mesmerized.

> *"I look as if I'd punch out your lights*
> *But I'm tired of all the trouble and fights.*
> *Give me a reason to calm my ways*
> *And I'll stop all the bashing, I means what I says."*

With the great beast hypnotized by Punky's pain-filled heart song, Mort was now left with the job of tying it up. Being submerged in the treacherous Salty Sea was bad enough – but being submerged with a beast like this was lunacy. Before he could chicken out, he grabbed the ball of wire and leaped in. He was going where no human had gone before – apart from Singrum Kelp (and we all know what happened to that poor sausage).

Mort plunged into the water and tried not to scream at the sight of the enormous arms that hung like weird chandeliers down into the deep. He started to swim round and round the rubbery mass and, whenever fear crept into his heart, he summoned the dark cloak of hate by telling himself: *Dad and Gosh and Gee are in the guts (or worse) of this terrible creature.* He worked hard, winding the wire and doing the best front crawl he'd ever done, binding the Belgo good and proper like a kipper parcel. It didn't protest, it didn't struggle – it was enchanted by the screaming song of the rock-crusher above.

Mort climbed back on board and stuck sponges in his ears while Punky sang on to keep the Belgo calm as they towed it home.

The rocky docks of Brutalia came into view and what a sight awaited them! The entire population of Brutalia had come to see the arrival of the Queen's *Golden Behind*, including the Queen (who thought it looked bigger than usual). The cheering made Mort feel like a hero. He even welcomed the pomp of the Royal Parp Horns.

The Belgo was helpless out of water – powerless

– and, as the guards heaved it on to dry land, Punky placed her arm round Mort's shoulder.

"I didn't think you had it in you, Mort the Meek. Maybe I should call you Mort the Murderer from now on!"

The words tiptoed like ice spiders down his spine. *Mort the Murderer*.

"Come on, let's be famous!" Punky yelled.

The crowds threw cabbages and crabs in the air to celebrate and Mort scanned the throng for faces he recognized. Mum! Scribe Pockle! The shin-kicking kids! Sally McRoot! And Weed.

Weed was the only one who wasn't smiling. Or throwing vegetables and crustaceans. He made a point of catching Mort's eye before he shook his head and turned away.

That's so out of character, Mort thought as he watched him go.

CHAPTER ELEVEN
THE WISE WOMAN

"Larry, where have you been? I haven't seen you all day!"

"I've been surfing."

"But you should be practising your dance steps, Larry."

"I wasn't surfing by choice. I got a bit tide up."

The Belgo lay spread out in the square, netted and hopeless. Its arms were still and its sorry eyes rolled with confusion as guards threw buckets of seawater over it to keep it alive. Because it wasn't allowed to die yet – not until the Grand God Feast. But until that event, to drum up excitement, everyone was encouraged to come and look. If they didn't, they'd get the **Punishment of the Day.**

PUNISHMENT OF THE DAY

*BOTTOM-SHUFFLE
ACROSS HOT COALS
AS GUESTS LAUGH
AT YOUR PAIN AT
THE GRAND GOD FEAST*

Crowds turned up but it had nothing to do with the threat of burnt bottoms. On that cruel island of Brutalia, teasing a large helpless animal was the next best thing to starting a fight. And, packed so closely together in the square, there was a good chance they'd have a crack at both.

Men and women chucked sticks and shouted rude

names, kids dared each other to tickle the arms and chefs sniffed it for inspiration. It was becoming a bit of a party. Then someone threw a punch and it really was a party. Everyone joined in, teasing the Belgo and punching each other on the nose. Everyone apart from Mort.

Calamari was about to be served with payback sauce. Mort should have been dancing round the Belgo, shouting, 'Yah-boo sucks to you!' and celebrating his revenge... So where was he?

Mort had fallen into a deep sleep, full of tossing and turning, with dreams of being locked in a sauna with a hundred hot, sweaty demons. For Mort's demons had not disappeared now that he had caught the Belgo. They had multiplied. And their breath had thickened, wrapping tightly round him, binding him like a Belgo's bad dream...

There was a knock at the door and Mort woke unsteadily from his nightmare. "Go away!" he shouted.

"Open up, it's the Queen," said a strange falsetto voice.

Mort had no choice. He crawled to the door and

opened it a fraction... But wait, that wasn't the Queen!

Weed Millet was too quick for Mort's slow reactions. He stuck his foot inside the door and forced his way in. "Hello, Mort."

"Hello." Mort got to his feet and folded his arms across his chest. His eyes roamed, looking anywhere but at his friend. It was as if their eyes were same-pole magnets, repelling each other. It felt really weird. Why were things so tense between them?

"I want to talk to you," Weed said.

"I've got nothing to talk about."

"Then, if you won't talk to me, I want you to talk to someone else."

"Who?"

"The Wise Woman."

"No way!"

People swore that going to see the Wise Woman had helped them with all sorts of problems, and Mort being so un-Morty was a very big sort of problem. Weed had to try. He had to reboot the Mort he knew and loved and get rid of this strange imposter. But would Mort allow himself to be re-Morted?

Weed held up a bag of his mum's freshly baked hot doughnuts. It was the sort of baking that only the Queen was allowed – unrotted and without fish-paste filling. Mort's tummy rumbled.

"OK then. But I want ALL the doughnuts."

Now, forget everything you think you know about wise people because it's worth mentioning that the Wise Woman wasn't actually wise. The whole mix-up was a problem with homophones.*

*Remember these? Homophones are words that sound the same like PEE and PEA. That's why spelling is important, which you'll know if you've ever ordered pee soup by mistake.

You see, the word WISE sounds a lot like the word WHYS (plural of why). And that's important.

WHY?

You'll see. Weed's Great-Aunt Quera Bulb, despite being one of the oldest people alive on Brutalia, had the conversational skills of a really annoying three-year-old.

WHY?

Exactly. It was never what, where, how or who. Just why.

WHY?

I don't know. It's just how her brain was wired.

WHY?

All right, now listen. There's only one person who asks WHY from now on and it's Quera Bulb because she's the WHYS WOMAN. She only became the **WISE WOMAN** because everyone on Brutalia was terrible at spelling and just assumed she had all the answers.

She never had answers. She only had one question.

WHY?

Precisely. But let's get back to the story and see what happens when you ask a simple question over and over again.

Warning: the word WHY might get annoying after a while, but just grit your teeth and get through this next scene ... and don't ask why.

Mort sat opposite the old and wrinkly Quera Bulb,

his face sullen. She stared at him with twinkly button eyes, waiting. She nodded several times encouragingly, but Mort didn't have a kipper's idea what to say.

Eventually Weed stepped forward. "Oh, Great Wise Woman Aunt, I have brought you my friend, Mort Canal, for he is troubled."

The Wise Woman, eyes pinned on Mort, said, "Why?"

"I don't know," mumbled Mort.

"Why?"

"I said I don't know."

"Why?"

"I can't explain."

"Why?"

"Because I've never felt this way before."

"Why?"

"Because before now I've always been peaceful and content."

"Why?"

"Because I've known my

own mind and my own emotions, and now I don't."

"Why?"

"Because I suddenly feel aggressive."

"Why?"

"Because the Belgo ate my family."

"Why?"

"Because it was hungry, I guess."

"Why?"

"Because it's an animal and animals eat to live."

"Why?"

"Because it's their instinct."

"Why?"

"Because that's all they know."

"Why?"

Mort didn't need to answer that. The last WHY was like a flash of clarity – like lightning zapping through the darkness. His head was clear as he bent down and clutched the old woman's hands. "Thank you, thank you. You truly deserve to be called the Wise Woman."

"Why?"

"Never mind. Come on, Weed. There's no time to lose!"

Mort felt alive, powered by the ferocious heartbeat of justice. We don't know what that is either, but it went:

BA-RUMP-PA-PUM-B-RUMP-PA-PUM.

Mort and Weed ran through the sordid side streets and blustery backstreets, wanting to whoop with the joy of friendship. But whooping would attract attention and they needed to talk. Somewhere private.

Privacy was important in Brutalia. Snit Parlot, the Royal Snoop, could be anywhere. Snit was notoriously nosy. He was also known to get the wrong end of the stick in his eagerness to return to the palace with titbits of gossip.

When he was sure the streets were clear of sneaks, Mort pulled Weed into a doorway and finally made eye contact, which was a really big moment.

"Thank you, Weed. You saved me."

"You're not saved yet," Weed said. "I feel as if there's trouble ahead."

(Weed can't tell the future – he's just been in one of these stories before.)

"Probably, but let me explain my revelation before we worry about what's to come. The Wise Woman was so wise. She forced me to ask myself some difficult questions, and it gave me the answer. It wasn't the Belgo I hated, it was me. I hated what I'd become. I let the demons of despair into my soul. I let my pain boil into bitterness and anger, and I stupidly thought that hurting something else would make me feel better."

"You were stretching the rules of the Pacifist Society of Brutalia," Weed said, shaking his head. "I'm not sure if you're still fit to be president actually."

"Do you know what Punky called me?" Mort said, ignoring Weed's comment.

"No."

"Mort the Murderer."

Mort the Murderer

The name looks horrible when written down, sounds horrible when heard and tastes horrible when spoken.

"Urgh! That's it, you definitely can't be president now," Weed tutted.

"But I'm *not* a murderer. The Belgo's not dead. Not yet. We have to release it."

"WE?"

"Yes, Weed. You're my best friend. We're doing this together."

"OK, thanks. LET'S FREE THE BELGO!"

"Shh, Weed! Snit Parlot might be listening."

CHAPTER TWELVE
PACIFISTS UNITE

"It's rehearsal time, Bruce!"

"Go on without me. I can't make it, Larry."

"Why not?"

"I've pulled a mussel."

Mort looked at the Belgo. Lying in the square under the moonlight, its arms were soft and squelchy, and its beautiful orange colour was fading like a satsuma in the sun. Its dead-looking eyes only glinted with the reflection of the fire. Because, all around the square, guards stood, holding flaming torches.

"What's going on? Why are there so many guards? What's with all the fire?" Weed whispered. *"Oh, I see... Look at the* **Punishment of the Day.***"*

PUNISHMENT OF THE DAY

TO BE DECIDED... BUT IT'S SERIOUSLY NASTY. ESPECIALLY FOR ANYONE THINKING OF FREEZING THE BELGO. SO DON'T DO IT.

"Snit Parlot must have heard us," Mort said. "Or misheard us. It looks like he told the Queen someone wanted to freeze the Belgo!"

"Freeing or freezing, it's makes no difference. With all those flaming guards standing about, there's no way we can help it escape. And, if we try to, we'll end up getting the Punishment of the Day. And it's seriously nasty." Mort slapped his thigh in frustration.

"Steady on, Mort. No slapping anyone, including yourself. Pacifist Promise, remember."

"You're right, Weed. I'm letting myself slip. Let's say the Pacifist Promise again to remind ourselves."

They closed their eyes and placed their hands on their hearts.

"I, a member of the Pacifist Society of Brutalia, promise not to hurt anything."

The boys hugged, but they were being watched by someone who wasn't into all that show your feelings stuff. Punky Mason stepped out of the shadows and moved closer. Her clothes were ripped as if she'd been in a fight with a combine harvester, and her eyes, which once shone like pale blue sapphires in a midnight sky, seemed as lifeless as old lettuce.

"Punky! Meet my friend, Weed Millet. Weed, this is Punky."

Punky brushed away the introduction and jabbed Mort in the chest. "Rumour is someone wants to freeze the Belgo. Better not be you, you snivelling water louse. If I don't get those blessings, you know what will happen, right?"

"You'll grind me into dust?"

"Yeah."

"Well, that's OK because I'm not freezing the Belgo. Why would I freeze the Belgo? Anyway, we can't hurt it now – we're saving that for the night of the Grand God Feast! **Mwa-ha-ha-he-hmmmm…**"

Mort's fake evil laugh didn't have the power of a real evil laugh, but Punky didn't notice. She seemed distracted. She prodded Mort again and walked away.

"Something's wrong," Mort said. "Her pokes are normally way more pokey."

They hid behind a pillar and watched her as she crossed the square. She stopped, quickly looked around and then dropped to her knees by the Belgo's head.

"What's she doing?" Weed whispered.

"Shh!" Mort had no idea, but there was something almost tender about the way Punky was leaning towards the beast. Really close, like she was smelling a rose.

Mort and Weed watched from the shadows, holding their breath. Was she delivering a hushed insult to the Belgo? A threat? Was she telling it that before the week was out it'd be speared and skewered and served up in a seafood broth?

Suddenly there was a sound – a bit like a washing machine being thrown down the stairs, where it crashed into a large cow, which then jumped through a windowpane.

Weed yelped and held his ears. "Urgh! What is that noise?"

"That's Punky singing. But look at the Belgo!"

As Punky sang, the Belgo's eyes unclouded and slid into focus. They looked at her longingly. The tips of its arms flicked and a stream of bubbles poured from its mouth, and then out came a sound. It dripped with pity and slime. It was singing.

"It's a duet!" Mort gasped.

They couldn't hear the words but it sounded something like this:

GLUB-BLUB BLURP
RAP SMASHER ROAR SO-THERE
GLUBBUB-BUBBLE-FLAM
KICKER GORILLA WAAAAH
DOUBLE-DECKER

When the duet had finished, Punky pressed her small eye against its massive eye and placed her hand momentarily on the distressed blob before snatching it back and running away.

"Well, that was weird," Weed said.

Their conversation was interrupted by the tip of a guard's spear. "Oi, are you kids going to be horrible to the beast or not? If not, then sod off."

"Let's sod off," Weed said.

"No, it'd be suspicious," Mort whispered. "Let's just say stuff that's not horrible in a horrible way."

Mort and Weed walked past the Belgo, yelling things that weren't horrible in a horrible way, so the guards wouldn't get suspicious.

"Beast of the sea, are you?
You're so big, you can't wear clothes
Ooh, you've got three arms.
Octopuses are sooooo salty!
You're magnificent, you are!"

WHAT?

The words had leaped out of Mort's mouth quite without planning. He didn't remember **thinking** those words, so they couldn't have come from his brain. They came from his HEART.

You're magnificent, you are...

Mort stared at the Belgo. And the Belgo stared at Mort, roused by his heartfelt compliment.

"Yes, you are magnificent," Mort said.

Magnificence shone through its slime like the glint of sun behind a cloud. There was only one other word for it – bathed in slippery splendour, the Belgo, dignified even as it was dying, was...

beautiful.

And, deep inside him, Mort felt a fierce stirring. Not like demons having a disco. More like a million butterflies taking flight, taking with them the weight that had been chained round his heart. It was *forgiveness. He was forgiving the Belgo.* Forgiving it for munching his family. And, by the time those butterflies had all flown, there wasn't an ounce of murderousness left in him. He wasn't setting free the Belgo just because he was a good pacifist. He wanted to free it because he *really wanted to* – so it could carry on living and being magnificent, a thing of sublime beauty in the treacherous Salty Sea.

"We need to do something!" he said, moving

his determination up a gear. "First, we must find somewhere Snit Parlot won't be lurking."

There was a scuffling sound up ahead as Snit Parlot tiptoed down a side alley. "Don't mind me," he said. "Just carry on talking. I'm not listening."

"Yes, you are," Weed said.

"No, I've gone now."

"But I can see your feet!"

Mort shook his head at Weed. Snit Parlot was not to be encouraged. He pointed towards the docks, and they slipped silently down the side streets where the crashing waves would drown out their voices.

The docks were eerie. There was only darkness, apart from the moon, which shone on the squabbling waves and illuminated a clutch of fishing boats. They swayed expectantly, loaded with nets and pulleys ready to go out to sea, to provide food for the Grand God Feast, no doubt. Apart from a few lobsters going through their steps, Mort and Weed were alone.

"What shall we do?" Weed said.

"I'm not sure," Mort said. He tossed a loose limpet into the sea, and there was a lump in his throat as he thought of the tragic limpet hunters, Dad and Gosh and Gee. But no anger followed. Just a sad little hiccup. "If we sit here quietly, something will come to us."

"I'm not very good at sitting quietly. I'll go and dance with the lobsters. Call me when you've thought of something." And Weed skipped away.

Mort sat alone on a rock and closed his eyes. He'd solved situations before – he knew that all he had to do was piece together a jigsaw. But first he had to catch the jigsaw pieces. He cast his mind like a net over the situation and went fishing ... and slithers of ideas, as quick as anchovies, darted in and out.

Punky loves the Belgo

The GRAND GOD FEAST

SUCKERS!

The ideas swam round and round, but they were fast and slippery. Mort couldn't net them – as quickly as one arrived, another vanished. He gritted his teeth and stretched his mind-net wider, determined to catch a little fishy thought. And then several ideas swam right into his trap. "Eureka!"

"It's not my fault," Weed called back, full of hurt. "Mum made me wash with squid paste again."

"No, Weed. I didn't say you REEK. I said EUREKA! It's means **'I've Found It'**.* I've found the answer!"

*It actually does mean this in Greek. This story is seriously amazing for your education.

Weed jumped up and down on the walkway, flicking lobsters back into the foamy sea. "Tell me, tell me!"

"What has this story been about so far, Weed?"

"God Queen ... Demi-God blessings... It's kind of been about gods, Mort."

"Yes, gods. Also suckers."

"Are you talking about octopus suckers or foolish suckers?"

"Octopus suckers, although Brutalia isn't short of foolish suckers. Look how many believe whatever the Queen tells us. When she said she was a god, we didn't even ask if it was true."

"Scribe Pockle has a document."

"Yes, he does. But the point is – no one asked to see it, did they? We all just believe what we're told most of the time. And that makes us proper suckers."

"So how is that going to help free the Belgo?"

Mort paused, his eyes twinkled and the ideas in his mind-net wriggled in anticipation...

"We say that killing the Belgo will anger a god."

"What god?"

"The one right in front of us."

"The Queen?"

"No. The Belgo. We say the Belgo is a god."

"That is GENIUS!"

The wind whistled and sea spray hissed and lobsters tutted as they climbed back on to the rickety planks. Mort and Weed said the Pacifist Promise, then high-fived and hugged. They were saviours.

Almost saviours. Saviours in spirit anyway.

"Mort, how do we convince the Queen that the Belgo is a god?"

Mort opened his mouth to speak and closed it again. Weed scratched his head. A dried-up urchin rolled between them like tumbleweed, and Mort's shoulders fell. Not far. Just enough to show he was a bit deflated.

"I knew there was a catch," he moaned. And the ideas in his net giggled, wriggled and escaped. They were gone. "The Belgo came from the sea. So it's there I should look for answers. There's nothing for it, Weed – I need to set sail for a Period of Contemplation."

"I'll come too. But we don't have a ship and I can only do front crawl for twenty-five metres before I sink."

"We don't need a ship," Mort said with a little smile. "We've got a *Big Susan*."

CHAPTER THIRTEEN
OUT TO SEA AGAIN

"Are lobsters supposed to dance, Larry?"

"We can do anything we put our minds to, Bruce."

"Anything?"

"Yes, you have to crab every opportunity in life."

The Pacifist Society of Brutalia was aboard a raft, heading out to sea. It meant that no one was left on the island to spread the message of peace. But sacrifices had to be made, and unless they came up with a plan the sacrifice would be a large sea creature that had only been doing what large sea creatures do and eating people. Nothing personal.

"Something's worrying me about Punky," Mort said as he swish-swashed the *Big Susan*. "She's about to become a god – about to escape her future as a reluctant rock-crusher – but she still seems so miserable."

"Wait until she finds out you're saving the Belgo and she's NOT going to be a god. She won't be miserable then. She'll be FURIOUS... She might even *kill* you, Mort."

"I hadn't thought of that," Mort said, biting his lip. "Maybe that's the price I have to pay for the bad things I've done."

"Oh, Mort."

"This could be the end for me. But I deserve it."

"Oh, Mort."

A wave then walloped them in the face, which put

salty water in their eyes so it looked as if they were crying. But they really were.

"I must be strong," Mort spluttered through another wave. "Because I'd rather die being Mort the Meek than live as **Mort the Murderer**."

"You're a GREAT pacifist," Weed sobbed through another mouthful of sea foam. "Don't die. Don't—"

And a series of huge waves came out of nowhere and smashed them in the face over and over like a relentless Grot Bear.

Something was disturbing the water. It was *weather*. *Bad* weather. As the seas whipped and stung, the friends held on to the *Big Susan* and prayed for their lives. They were tossed around and their cries were ripped from their mouths by swell after swell of face-thwacking water.

"Mort, it's—"

SPLOOSH

"I can see a—"

SPLASH

"In the distance—"

CRASH

"A boat—"

SMOOSH

Mort, fearing that their story might end too soon if they were swallowed up in the vicious grey chop, did something out of character (even though he'd fallen back *into* character). He got to his feet, surfing the *Big Susan* as she buckaroo-ed on the angry wash, held up his arms to the sky and yelled:

"MAKE IT STOP!"

And it did.

The wind instantly died and the waters dropped to a gentle sway. It was as if the storm had never existed. Weed, who had tumbled and rolled to the other side of the *Big Susan*, crawled back on hands and knees and wrapped his arms round Mort's legs like an adoring squid. "Mort, you saved us."

Then on the breeze came the call of a hundred men and women.

"AHOY THERE!" (x 100)

Sailing towards them were, let's say, thirty-five boats. They circled the *Big Susan* and dropped anchor. Mort and Weed were locked in, caught like fish in a net. Weed clung to Mort. "What are we going to do? We can't fight that many at once."

"We can't fight that many at all. We're pacifists, remember?"

"Oh yeah."

"We shall hold out our arms to show we're not carrying any weapons."

"But then we'll be an easy target!"

"We have no choice. Are you a pacifist or not?"

It was the first time, since earlier, that there had been tension between them. Weed needed to search his soul. Searching your soul is something you have to go on a Journey of Contemplation for, but as he was already on one that speeded things up a bit.

"I've given it some thought, Mort. And I AM a pacifist through and through."

"Glad to hear it," Mort said.

The Pacifist Society of Brutalia then opened its four arms and, just as Weed predicted, it made them an easy target. But the stuff being chucked at them was not weaponry. It was flowers!

Mort and Weed froze in confusion (where had these people found flowers at sea?) as an enormous man with a rose in his teeth shimmied down a rope ladder and landed on the *Big Susan* with a thud. He was thoroughly tattooed with muscles the size of baby cows and a full fisherman's beard matted with small crabs. He fell to his knees, placing the rose at Mort's feet. "Oh, Weather God, we thank you for sparing our vessels."

"Sorry, what?" Mort said, startled.

"OH, WEATHER GOD, WE THANK YOU
FOR SAVING OUR VESSELS!" he shouted.

"I'm not the God of the Weather."

"Yes, you are."

"I think you're mistaken."

"YES, YOU ARE!" he yelled. "We saw you
command the storm to stop."

"It was a coincidence," a voice piped up. It was a
fisherwoman called Barb. "That's what I told him,"
she said.

"Thank you!" Mort said, nodding.

"No, you told it to stop and it did."

"It was just a squall," Mort said. "A sudden gust
that dies away as quickly as it comes. They're quite
common at sea."

"Just what I told him!" Barb shouted. "Bert,
you're a berk."

"No. You are a god. I've decided that you are,"
Bert said solemnly. "And we, the Fisherfolk's
Cooperative of Luncheon Island, would like to give
you our thanks. Fisherfolk, bring your gifts."

Fisher people from the giant Fisherfolk's

Cooperative of Luncheon Island poured down their rope ladders and on to the *Big Susan* with gifts of the finest tunas, sea bass, lobsters and scallops. Then they all began chanting, apart from Barb, who shook her head.

"We thank you, oh Weather God, divine, windy Weather God. God of all things meteorological."

Then they waved their arms a bit before falling on their faces and chanting it over again. And again. And again.

Weed was transfixed. He looked first at the worshippers and then at Mort, then back at the worshippers and again at Mort, as if deciding who to believe.

"Just because lots of people believe something, that doesn't make it true, Weed."

"You say that, but I'm not sure... You *are* quite special, Mort."

"Look, it was just a squall," Mort implored. "It was a SQUALL!"

"I know," Barb tutted. "But you'd better say something or this lot will be here all day and fish don't catch themselves, you know."

Mort coughed to get everyone's attention and his congregation fell silent. Bert shuffled closer, waiting for his Weather God's divine words to drop. For Barb's sake, and for the sake of the Journey of Contemplation, Mort decided to go along with it.

"Fisherfolk's Cooperative of Luncheon Island, you are very kind," Mort said.

Their voices – one hundred of them – rose as one:

"No, YOU are very kind."

Being adored was more awkward than Mort had

ever imagined.

"You must go now and, er, may the weather of the Salty Sea be good to you."

Bert got to his feet and took Mort's hand.

"You have been kind to us, Weather God. If there's anything we can do for you, let us do it. ANYTHING. ANYTHING AT ALL. ANYTHING, ALL RIGHT?"

"Anything, all right?"
(x 100)

"Er, yes. Thank you. Although you've already been nice, what with all the fish and stuff. There's enough there for a grand feast."

Mort thought about the biggest grand feast of all – the God Feast, where the Queen would be entertaining her suitors and feeding them the best vegetables from the land and the finest fruits of the sea: morsels ordinary Brutalians could only dream of.

Wait! What was that? Morsels? No, go back a bit. Back a bit more... That's it! There it was, another idea in the mind-net. Mort examined his catch. He liked what he saw. His face lit up and Weed noticed.

"What is it, oh Weather God?"

"Stop it, Weed. I've just found the answer to the big catch."

"What, this big catch?" Weed pointed at the pile of fish at their feet.

"No – the big catch! The problem of how to make the Queen believe the Belgo is a god."

After discussions with the Cooperative, Mort and Weed swish-swashed back towards Brutalia, wanting to laugh, but not sure if they should. After all, it was only an idea. Would it work? Only a god could tell you that and, after much persuasion and some basic explanations about shipping forecasts, Weed agreed that Mort wasn't a god.

"I don't know why you pretended to be one then," he tutted.

Mort shook his head and tried not to laugh.

CHAPTER FOURTEEN

NOTHING FISHY GOING ON AT ALL

"Have you noticed something strange about the sea?"

"I can't see any fin."

"Precisely. The fish have all gone."

Mort was woken from a long and turbulent sleep by a furious thumping.

"What's that furious thumping?" he called.

"It's me, chucking cooking pots at the wall. They called me a slime-bucket. *Again!*" his mum yelled.

"No, not that thumping. The other thumping."

Was it Punky, ready to grind him into dust? Was it creepy Snit Parlot, adoring Bert or someone else who had got the wrong end of the stick? Fear now roamed round Mort's stomach like someone down the vegetable market looking for a fight.

Mort got up and opened the door, just a teeny-tiny bit, and squished his eyeball against the crack.

It was Weed, jumping up and down like he needed the loo. His little face grinned and his wide chocolate-button eyes twinkled like those of a woodland creature. "It's happening," he said.

They raced down the smelly side streets and bellicose backstreets of Brutalia, not caring if their feet squelched in nasty-looking puddles. They had to get to the square. Things were kicking off.

The Queen was really putting the Highness in Royal Highness this time. Sitting on a wooden chair balanced precariously on very high stilts, she was closer to the sky than she'd ever been before. And she was cross. Very cross. The target of her fury was Brutalia's fisherfolk.

"What do you mean there are no fish?" she cried. "You are fishing people, are you not?"

A fisherman called Spat Mackerel stepped forward and craned his neck to look up at her.

"Yes, we are fishing people. But, if there aren't any fish in the sea, we can't catch them."

"No fish in the sea? Don't be ridiculous!"

"It's true, your very high Royal Highness," said Spat. "We haven't caught a single fish since we began fishing yesterday evening."

"Apart from a hard herring," said a fishergirl called Finn.

"Yeah, we do have a hard herring," Spat said, holding up the stiff little fish.

"You have WHAT?"

"We have a hard herring!" Spat shouted.

"Yes, I heard you the first time. But I can't feed a hundred of the Salty Sea's most eligible bachelors on a HARD HERRING! **It's not good enough,"** she yelled. "Does anyone have any ideas?"

"I could make some soup," called Sally McRoot. "I've got three potatoes; real special they are. Look like bums."

"Potato-bum soup?" the Queen screamed. "I can't give my future king potato-bum soup!"

She yelled for her Chief Guard. "Enot Stone! You've got a name that is the same backwards and forwards so you must be clever. Tell me what we should do?"

Enot, whose name was cleverer than him, stepped forward. "Well, you see ... um ... ah ... er..."

Spat Mackerel saved him from any more agony. "It's simple. We need to work out *why* there are no fish. If we find that out, then we can make them come back again."

The Queen spat at Spat. "Why then?"

"Dunno, never seen anything like it."

"Anyone? Anyone at all have any idea why our seas contain not a single fish, apart from a small hard herring?" the Queen shrieked.

There was a vast silence, full of people not knowing. Rotten potatoes rolled like lumpy tumbleweed across the square. Ravens stopped mid-peck. Kids stopped stealing things. A small hard herring held its breath. The Queen's face looked like it might explode.

Weed nudged Mort. "Now?"

Mort shook his head. A little bit longer...

A little bit longer...

A little bit longer...

The air trembled and the Queen's face exploded like a bath bomb into a million colours. Mort slowly raised his hand. "I think I know why, divine Queen."

The Queen narrowed her eyes and beckoned him closer. "The Belgo catcher. Tell me."

"We have angered the Fish God."

"Angered the Fish God?"

"Yes, angered the Fish God."

"Angered the Fish God?"

Mort supressed an eye-roll. "Yes!
I believe that we have angered the Fish
God and the Fish God has commanded that
no fish swim within three miles of Brutalia."

"That's very specific," the Queen said suspiciously.

"It's just a guess."

"Where is this Fish God then?"

"It's right here." Mort pointed to the Belgo, which was now ash grey.

"THAT is the Fish God?"

"Yes, I knew there was something divine about it when we caught it. It was glowing and magical and really very special. And now look. Its colour has faded, its life is draining and, when it dies, I wouldn't be surprised if the very last little hard herring dies with it."

But the Queen wasn't falling for it that easily. "How can you be sure?"

"A hunch," Mort said.

"Right, well, a hunch is a pretty good sign," the Queen conceded. "So, if we release the Belgo, the fish will return in time for the Grand God Feast?"

"Yes, the fish will return in abundance. And as thanks to you – our God Queen – the Fish God will surely see you as a friend."

"Nice touch," Weed whispered.

"What was that all about?"

The yell was like a bulldog chewing a bucket and spade.

It was inevitable. It was angry. It was Punky Mason. And she was throwing stuff. A shower of gravel bounced off Mort's head, followed by a sizeable rock.

"Ouch!"

"You deserve so much more than ouch," she growled, stamping towards him. "You deserve eternal pain for what you've done. You've lost me everything. You tricked me—"

But her tirade was interrupted.

"Stand aside! Stand aside for the Queen's Guard!"

Marching guards escorted a huge crowd made up of Brutalia's burliest men and women. They were carrying the enormous greying Belgo down to the docks. Its body and arms slopped and sorry gobs of slime dripped like custard. But no one complained about the goop in their hair and the gunk in their ears. They were carrying a Fish God and, if anything happened to it, there would be years of seafood famine and a vindictive Queen up their nostrils making up punishments every hour.

Punky's eyes followed the procession. Her face crumpled and scrunched and she made strange noises as she watched her ticket to Godville disappear. But wait – there was something confusing about the way she snarled and spluttered. Something mysterious about the way she growled and rasped. Something really odd about the way she scooped some Belgo slime and ran it through her short hair, making it spike upwards like a stiff brush. She turned to Mort.

Never before had she looked so fierce, with her piercings and urchin hair, and the coal-dust streaks that ran in rivers of frustrated tears down her cheeks.

Her eyebrows knitted together. "Where do you want to die, you disgusting pile of sea sludge?"

"Punky, you're really confusing me. One minute I think you want to kill the Belgo and the next it looks like—"

"Looks like I'll rip your head off," she spat, placing her huge (and surprisingly soft) hands round his neck.

Weed ducked under and popped his head up between her arms. "Now, let's just calm down."

"It's little weedy Weed! The weediest shrimp of them all." Punky let go of Mort and grabbed Weed by the hair. But Weed didn't whimper. He whipped out his confidence and his best voice and spoke in a rather magnificent way.

"I'm Weed, all right. I'm Weed Millet, member of the Pacifist Society of Brutalia and I won't let you fight. Violence is for people who don't have any other way of expressing themselves."

Punky raised her fist. "What do you expect? I'm a rock-crusher, like my mother – may she rest in pieces – and my father, and all their mothers and fathers before that. It's what I am. I don't do other ways of expressing myself."

That's not right, Mort thought. And a plucky idea darted across his brain. He grabbed for it with his net... His mind was racing, his eyes dancing with excitement. Plans were forming. Ideas swimming upstream towards the net. All he needed was some time.

~~Freeze~~ Free the Belgo

It's what I am...

Mort took Punky's face in his hands and stared into her icy blues. When he spoke, he was as cool as a cucumber ice cube. "You can have your revenge. You can stone me, tattoo me, pierce me, kick me, grind me into dust if you want. But give me a day. One day to make you change your mind."

"Can I tattoo BUM on your head before I kill you?"

Mort wondered briefly if she was related to bum-shaped vegetable enthusiast, Sally McRoot. "Yes, anything."

Punky gave one long last look at a trailing arm

of the Belgo before rubbing her wet eyes. Then she walked away.

"Don't look at me like that, Weed." Mort tried to ignore his friend's big, worried, chocolatey eyes, which glooped with concern. But it was tricky. They were kind of sticky. "Look, I'll work something out. But right now we need to make sure the Belgo gets back in the water, and then..."

"All aboard the *Big Susan*?" Weed's voice wobbled at the thought of another trip to the queasy Salty Sea. And, although Mort's stomach, eyes and teeth ached at the thought, he couldn't give up now. They were so close. But he'd let Weed off – the boy had turned grey. Mort quickly pepped up his voice to sound enthusiastic.

"Yes, it's time to go and see Bert and Barb and the Fisherfolk's Cooperative of Luncheon Island. But I need you to stay here, Weed."

"What for?"

"I want you to watch Punky. From a safe distance."

CHAPTER FIFTEEN
GOD SPEED

*"I've hurt myself, Larry. I'm worried
I won't be able to dance properly."*

"Which part of you."

"The pincer."

"Well, that is claws for concern..."

The boats of the Fisherfolk's Cooperative of Luncheon Island were dotted three miles out to sea in a circle round Brutalia. And, between the boats, there were fishing nets holding back an enormous tide of sea creatures. (Including one lobster that was late for dance practice.)

The *Big Susan* flopped steadily towards Bert and Barb, who stood at the prow of their boat, covered in tattoos and crabs. "Ahoy there!" Mort shouted.

And a joyful chorus returned.

"AHOY THERE!" (x 100)

Bert bowed and curtseyed and saluted and got in quite a muddle with his worshipping. "God of the Weather, we did as you requested. We held the fish back from Brutalia. I don't know why you wanted such a strange thing, but who am I to question a god! I'm a big fan."

"He really is a big fan," Barb said, rolling her eyes. "Go on, show him, Bert."

Bert grinned and rolled up his trouser leg
to reveal a large thigh tattoo of Mort's face.
"What do you think? Barb did it."

"I think it's, er, very nice. Thank you, Bert."

"So, what can I do for you now?"

"I want you to let the fish go free."

"What's the point in that?" Barb scoffed.

Bert nudged her. "He will have his reasons!
Oh, God of the Weather, of course we will let the
fish go free. Really, though? All of them?"

"Yes, please."

"Wait a minute." Bert shuffled off and returned
a moment later with armfuls of petals. "Just one
last time, yeah?"

Bert showered Mort with flowers as Barb
muttered, "Bonkers," under her breath, and
Mort tried very hard not to laugh. But there was
something about those flowers – so vibrant and
lush. Not like anything you'd find on Brutalia
or indeed on any of the Salty Sea islands, apart
from—

"Bert and Barb, you haven't been to Dead

Man's Island, have you?"

"Oh yeah, we're regulars there," Barb replied. "We like to visit the flower market and stop for a nice pawpaw juice once in a while. Why?"

"Just wondering," Mort said, smiling as he remembered an old friend called Ono, who had grey hair and cloudy eyes and grew the most exotic blossoms on that strangely named rock. He would have loved to have sat and talked about that dreamy place all day, but time was ticking and a Belgo was waiting. "I'd better go now, Bert. If you could do your thing?"

Bert signalled to the next boat in his fleet, which signalled to the next and the next, etcetera. And they all prepared to drop their nets and release the enormous ache of underwater animals that was straining at every cord, desperate to swim free.

"It's been a pleasure to know you, Weather God," Bert said. "Let's count down..."

THREE

"Pleasure to know you too, Bert," Mort said. "Bye, Barb."

TWO

"Bye," she said, dropping her voice to a whisper. *"That tattoo – I drew it on with a biro. It'll wash off after a while."*

ONE

"Thank you all for—"

WHOOSH!

The *Big Susan* flew through the air, with Mort standing at its helm like the captain of a fabulous flying carpet. It was a fairy tale in motion, and even Mort had to admit he felt quite godlike. Just for a bit.

"Look how he's commanded those fish to carry him!" sighed Bert, who was full of admiration, but not very full of observations. It's a good job his wife loved science.

"Don't be daft, Bert. It's what happens when you hold back a tide," Barb tutted. "It rushes forward all at once. A bit like when you held back that far—"

Barb was thwacked by a stray mugfish headed in the wrong direction. By the time she got to her feet, Mort and the *Big Susan* had been carried out of sight.

The wave of fish eventually lost energy, and after a while Mort found himself bobbing along again, carried only by the gentle wash of the ocean. Apart from the occasional creak as he yanked the swish-swash, it was peaceful. Perfect for some top-notch contemplation.

After all the action, Mort would have loved to have carried on cruising, sunbathing and sucking on seaweed, but there was no time for that – he had saved the Belgo, but now he needed to save himself from Punky. He had to get his ideas all in a line. There were things to be done and songs to be sung... A plan started hatching in Mort's head.

First, and most important, was convincing Punky Mason not to kill him. He had one day – just twenty-four hours – to save himself from being ground into dust or stoned to death or buried alive under a boulder. He knew that's how rock-crushers did things. But was Punky really a rock-crusher? She might have been by birth, and she knew all the right rock-crushing words, but her heart wasn't in it. She wanted more from life than that. And this had to be the key to salvation. *THINK!* Mort told himself.

THINK for your life! But he couldn't think, because of his second thought...

Songs to be sung.
Songs to be sung... Songs to be sung...

"OK, so there are songs that need to be sung!" Mort shouted at the sky, although it wasn't the sky's fault. After a quick apology to the blameless blue, he asked, "What songs?"

As the raft listed on the waves, Mort also listed:

Nursery rhymes?

Show songs?

Rude songs?

Pacifist songs?

Heart songs?

Wait! Heart songs! That's it. HEART SONGS! WHOOOOO-HOOOOO!

Finally, his ideas – like regimental anchovies – were all in a line.

CHAPTER SIXTEEN
THE BELGO'S MELODY

"What are you doing, Larry? We're late for the show!"

"Just a minute, I'm having a seawee."

"If we don't hurry up, we'll really be in hot water."

"You crack me up, Bruce."

Mort darted between the doorways and shadows, running fast and keeping low. The warm, doughy smell of his best friend's house hit him as he rounded the corner and he skidded to a halt outside the Millets' door. He knocked lightly. The door swung open and standing there was a little girl holding a doll made out of bread. She bit off its head.

"Hi, Semolina. Is your brother in?"

Semolina – who had a voice so small no one knew if she was talking or just pretending to be a mouse – squeaked.

"Was that a 'yes' or a mouse?" Mort asked patiently, but he didn't have to wait to find out. Before you could say, "Whoa there!", he found himself wrapped up in a huge pacifist hug.

"Mort!" Weed said, finally letting go. "You're back!"

"Yes, I am. It took ages. Some of the streets are closed off. The whole of Brutalia is being cleaned. You'd hardly recognize the place – there's no disease-filled puddles or poo piles anywhere. But Mum says they'll probably put the mud and dung back once the visitors have gone. So, do you want to hear the news?"

"No need to tell me – I already know! Dad had a banquet meeting at the palace and he said there was seafood everywhere. Everywhere! It looks like everything's tied up good and proper like a kipper parcel."

"Not so fast, Weed. There are more things to tie up before we can celebrate, and I'm not talking about kipper parcels. Did you follow Punky while I was gone?"

"Yes, yes, I did, and she was acting most peculiarly. She was crying. Properly crying, with her mouth wide open. I could even see her uvula! I was surprised to see it wasn't pierced, to be honest."

"Oh dear. Anything else?"

"She's dyed her hair bright orange. Now it's spiky and orange."

"Interesting... Anything else?"

"She followed a cockroach and screamed at it."

"Are you sure it was screaming?"

"It sounded like ships smashing into rocks and rocks smashing into ships."

"Weed, that wasn't screaming. It was singing.

I've come up with a plan to persuade Punky not to kill me, and this last bit of information is exactly what I wanted to hear. Punky is trying to get herself a pet."

The rubble tip was hard and rocky, full of sharp edges and blunt weapons. It was dangerous being here when someone *didn't* want to kill you. Mort gulped, just as he had done when he first met Punky. But he had to be brave.

Punky was at the far end of the tip – a dark silhouette against a gloomy sky. She was picking up boulders but, instead of hurling them to the ground to break them apart, she let them fall gently at her feet. Block-smashing had never looked so sad.

Mort took a step closer. Another one. Then another one. And then she turned, a little too late, because he was right there.

"What's the Time, Mr Wolf!" he said with a nervous laugh.

"Sod off," she muttered.

"You're not going to kill me then?"

"Oh yeah. Where do you want to die?" Her voice was as limp as a rat with a poorly foot.

"Follow me."

Mort led her along the dizzyingly high cliffs of Brutalia until they reached a rock that jutted out impossibly and precariously from the land mass.

This was the lugging rock, where Brutalia's dead were once thrown into the sea. That was before the father of Mort's mysterious friend Ono started taking the bodies to Dead Man's Island instead. Mort hiccuped as he thought of his father and Gosh and Gee, robbed of the chance of a burial on Ono's wonderful island of flowers. But he had to stay strong.

He walked Punky to the very edge of the rock. Directly below it, the turbulent spume roared.

"Are you telling me you want to die here?" Punky snarled, flaring a studded nostril. "Shoving people off cliffs isn't my style. I'm a crusher, you know."

"Punky, I've been thinking about that—"

Just then, Enot Stone and two guards appeared and Punky clenched her fists. "Good one, clam-puke –

looks like you've got us in trouble."

"I asked them to come," Mort whispered. "Just let me do the talking."

The guards halted and shouted some words nobody understood (along the lines of HYAAAAAH HOH!).

From behind Enot Stone, the Queen appeared. "What is this?" she demanded.

Mort cleared his throat. "Your Majesty, this rock-crusher, Punky Mason, has a special connection with the Belgo – the Fish God."

"Is this true?"

"Yes, it's true. And now you can tell your suitors that not only have you caught the Fish God – not only have you released the Fish God – not only has it rewarded you with a magnificent catch – but, with Punky's help, you have tamed it too. Who in the Salty Sea could ever have imagined that this monstrous octopus would ever be under anyone's spell? That's real power. Better than any trophy. And definitely worthy of a Demi-God blessing, don't you think?"

Mort turned to Punky, whose eyes had begun swimming. "I don't know what's going on," she sobbed. Her lips were trembling.

"Make your voice tremble too," he encouraged. "Punky – that rock is your stage. And out there beneath the waves is your audience. Your friend. Your Belgo."

Mort stepped back and Punky opened her mouth. Noise poured out.

"What the heck is THAT?" the Queen shrieked, cupping her ears. "It sounds like Grot Bears eating a dentist!"

"It's a song."

The Queen was about to protest and possibly get a guard to push them both into the sea, but her eyes were suddenly drawn to the ocean below. It had started to bubble furiously. Beneath the boiling white, the water took on a deep orange hue and the dome of the Belgo emerged from the froth. The tips of its three arms drew themselves up from the deep and waved at Punky. The splendid creature bobbed in the wash, half in, half out, its eyes fixed on the girl on the rock high above. Quite marvellously hypnotized by her ear-shredding song.

Mort walked to the edge and stood beside Punky, not caring if her voice made his brain bleed. He watched her face, saw her eyes twinkling like the sun on water, and her mouth curling at the edges. Not a snarl but a smile.

"It loves you, Punky," Mort said softly as her song came to an end.

She turned, sniffed and nodded. "Thank you, Mort. This is a perfect scene to end on, don't you think?"

"Not yet!" the Queen yelled. "No one leaves this story until I've found my King and I get my happy-ever-after. Punky, come to the feast to receive your Demi-God blessing. Bring a friend if you must. Enot! Guards! Lead the way."

When the royal bunch had gone, Punky and Mort looked down at the Belgo playing in the sea. It was juggling fishing boats and blowing raspberries.

"I think your pet's showing off," Mort laughed.

"He doesn't look it, but he's a total softy!" she said. "No one would believe me if I told them."

"Once you have a reputation, it's hard to shake, isn't it, Punky?" They exchanged meaningful looks and then Punky laughed so hard you could see her uvula. Mort was pleased to see it still wasn't pierced.

Bad reputations. Punky and the Belgo were like peas in a pod. The only difference was that Punky had *given herself* a reputation as a defence, and the Belgo's reputation was all because of fear. Perhaps it did eat people, but so did salty sharks given half the chance, and, apparently, giant Brutalian crabs.

Before Singrum Kelp's sob story, the Belgo was probably just like any other sea creature. Singrum had made it sound as if the Belgo had tortured him on purpose, but who knew if Singrum's wounds had anything to do with the Belgo in the first place? The fact is no one had ever questioned Singrum's story, and people believe anything when it's written down.

The Belgo cartwheeled through the waters below – the big show-off – and Mort wondered if it even ate humans at all. There was no proof that it did. No one had seen it with their own eyes. Maybe there was a chance that his dad and Gosh and Gee… His hopeful thoughts were suddenly interrupted by a recollection of Scribe Pockle's scroll and all those words about

the Beadly Deast – with its muddled-up **B**s and **D**s.
And suddenly thoughts hula-hooped round and round
inside his head.

People believe anything when it's written down ...

"Punky, I've got to go!"

"Why?"

"Because I think my brain is trying to tell me
something fishy is going on. And I need to go and visit
an ancient man for a game of Rock, Paper, Scissors."

CHAPTER SEVENTEEN

FEAST YOUR GODS

"Sorry I made us miss the show, Bruce."

"That's okay, Larry. Turns out it was a good job we did miss the show."

"Did it go badly?"

"Let's just say it wasn't the shellabration we thought it was going to be."

The docks were filled with solid ships that really were solid. They belonged to the Salty Sea's finest single men of noble birth. Barons and earls and poshos. Most of them had come to check out the God Queen and have a quick nose round the curiously cut-off island of Brutalia. Others had come for the seafood because gossip had exploded and scuttled across the Salty Sea islands like popcorn crabs. "A Fish God has given Brutalia the gift of abundance. Pass it on."

And now all those greedy poshos were seated at an enormous banqueting table. It stretched the length of the palace hall and sat no fewer than 103, including the Queen, her suitors, her palace officers and two very special civilians.

Punky and Mort stared round at everyone who had dressed ridiculously for the occasion. There were frills and buttons and ribbons and billowing britches, like puff pastries – and a few looked like they'd rolled through a sewing shop in a Velcro onesie.

The Queen's attire wasn't ridiculous. It was **revolting**. She had embellished her eyebrows with hairy caterpillars and she wore a long dress embroidered with fish scales to make her glitter in a Godly Fashion. They also made her stink like a haddock's swimming costume.

Mort and Punky didn't really know what to make of it all. It wasn't really their scene, but their awkward silence was swallowed by show-offy men talking loudly about their wealth (and exclaiming, "*Poo-wee*, what's that smell!"). Then suddenly a gong was bonged, and the hall fell silent.

The Queen got to her feet. The rustling of her smelly dress caused the three nearest barons to faint. "Gentlemen, I hope you have enjoyed the day so far. The belching pigs, the Grot Bear boxing and those marvellous dancing lobsters, which you will have the benefit of tasting in the third course..."

In the corner, a guard (and part-time dance instructor) broke down and was led out screaming. The gong had to be bonged again to restore order. And then the room was so quiet you could hear an oyster pop.

The Queen paused, eyes glittering with glory. "But now the entertainment is over..."

"What about the bun dance?" piped up a posho.

"I was told that there'd be a bun dance."

Confusion reigned until the problem was identified. Indeed, a **bun dance** and **abundance** were easily mixed up (although the pastry-obsessed Posho Crotchly of Squadge Island was so disappointed he left before the first course).

"BUT NOW THE INTERESTING PART!" the Queen shrieked, quickly popping on a fake smile. Blotches of impatience were creeping up her neck. "We have reached the bit about ME! As you all know, it has been discovered that I come from a family of GODS."

There was polite applause, and Mort caught the eye of an ancient man sitting a few seats down. They stared at each other for a while before the Queen's shrill voice cut through their silent communication.

"Not only am I a GOD, I am a GOD with friends in high places. The FISH GOD is a good friend of mine and he has provided us with an abundance of food for this occasion. Not a bun dance. Not a barn dance. ABUNDANCE. The Fish God loves me, you see."

Punky pinched Mort's knee under the table and lowered her voice.

"What a cheek!"

"Shh, Punky."

The Queen continued. "And later this night, before you leave, I will summon him to the shores to wave you goodbye. I have him almost literally in the palm of my hand."

Punky pinched Mort's knee even harder.

"The Belgo is not her pet," she hissed.

"Shh. As long as she's not hurting anything, let her have her way."

"And now, rich gentlemen and poshos of the Salty Sea, eat and be merry, and be very, very flirty. Because, by the end of the lobster course, I shall have chosen my King. And over pudding we shall celebrate with marriage. Waiters, bring the food!"

Waiters filed into the banqueting hall and the steam of a hundred hot dishes filled the air. The Queen puckered her lips, raised her caterpillars, and her fake laugh crackled through the smoky atmosphere, torturing the ears of every suitor who had them, and insulting the intelligence of those with a brain.

Some of the suitors did have ears and brains as it

turns out. So, when the steam evaporated and the air cleared, it was apparent that the banqueting table was half empty.

"Where have they gone?" the Queen shrieked. "Where are my suitors?"

"Stuff them!" came a rich voice.

The owner of the rich voice leaped on to the table, kicking aside lobsters and spilling wine. He was handsome and tall, with eyes that danced like ferrets at a hoedown. He raised a thick eyebrow and then bowed low to the Queen.

"Your DIVINE Majesty, those were men who would rather run than lose. They were cowards. Too spineless, too weak to stand by such a strong woman. Only one man here is bold enough to be your King."

"What a load of rubbish," Punky spat. "They left because they

realized she's an irritating sea slug."

"I thought I was the sea slug," Mort said.

"I changed my mind."

The Queen beckoned the brave man closer. "And your name is?"

"Bilious Pretender of Jaundice Island, Your Majesty. Bill to my friends."

The Queen cast her eyes at the remaining suitors. Bilious Pretender was the only one who wasn't asleep or vomiting and didn't look like an old leather punchbag. Her mind was made up. She picked up a plate and threw it at the wall to get everyone's attention.

"I have chosen my King!" she declared. The others didn't look that disappointed. "Bilious Pretender is handsome and strong. I am gorgeous and goddessy. We are a match made in heaven. We shall join together and the islands of Jaundice and Brutalia will become one."

"Er, that's not physically possible," said Inko Carter, the Queen's map-maker. "They're islands, you see."

"Well, you'll have to work something out. Or you can accidently fall off a cliff. Up to you!"

Bilious Pretender of Jaundice Island laughed and laughed as if his bride-to-be had magnificent wit.

"He's worse than she is!" Punky said.

"They're well suited then," Mort replied. "I bet he

doesn't care about her or Brutalia..."

"Bring the marriage course!" the Queen shrieked, clapping with excitement as Bill flung himself into a chair next to her, plugged his nostrils with bread and snuffled her neck. She giggled. It was horrible.

The doors of the palace hall rattled and waiters paraded the pudding platters – seafood profiteroles piled high like stacked fish balls (because that's what they were). As the fish balls were being served, the Queen had the gong bonged once more. It was the signal. The signal for the marriage bit to begin, which started with the dismissal of the current King.

Enot brought him in and what a sorry sight the King was, so dazed and confused. He had been sitting round the back of the palace for days, bored out of his wits.

"Ah, my King. *Darling*—" the Queen said out of habit.

"He's not your king and he's not your darling. Not any more," interrupted Bilious.

"Absolutely right. Old King, you are hereby replaced by Bilious Pretender of Jaundice Island and I command you to leave Brutalia and find a new home."

"Not so fast," boomed Bilious. "A dethroned king cannot be exiled."

"Maybe he is good after all," Punky whispered.

Bilious thumped the table. "He must be executed."

"I take that back..."

"Ex-ex-execution?" the Queen stuttered.

Bilious Pretender fixed his thick eyebrows in a deep scowl and glared at her with fire and passion. "It's the dawn of a new era, is it not? You are no longer merely a Queen. You are a God Queen. And gods need to do a bit of brutal stuff – it's tradition."

The Queen nodded slowly, but Mort thought he saw a slight flicker in her eye. Was it regret? Worry? Panic? Either way, he had to do something. And that something was already planned for this exact moment – the moment where a harmless little misprint on an old document got turned into a big fat crime. It was time to tell the truth. He stood up, threw his plate at the wall for attention and shouted,

"OBJECTION!"

"Who is that little shrimp?" Bill said, narrowing his sneaky eyes.

"For the last time, it's WIMP!" (It wouldn't be the last time.) "And this wimp is Mort the Meek, President of the Pacifist Society of Brutalia. I am here to fight violence wherever I find it on this humble island. And, right now, I don't like what I see."

"Who cares? You're just a weird kid. My Queen can do whatever she likes to whomever she likes because she's a bloomin' GOD. Come on, Queenie, let's chop this old King's head off and get on with it, shall we? SHALL WE?"

The old King whimpered. The Queen most definitely gulped.

It was time for some hard truths. Mort nodded at the ancient Scribe Pockle sitting a few seats down, who slowly rose to his feet.

"I'm afraid there has been a mistake," Scribe said. "We were going to let it ride, but things have gone too far."

"Mistake? What mistake?" Bilious Pretender growled.

Scribe Pockle continued, unflustered. "Old scrolls were written in a peculiar time when not much attention was given to spelling and grammar..."

"GET ON WITH IT!" Bilious shouted biliously.

"I am getting on with it," Scribe said. "As I was saying, in those days writing was quite muddled. For instance, the **B**s and **D**s were often reversed."

"AND, AND, AND?" Bill spat.

"And it seems that the present King was not descended from a Dank Empire, but a **Bank** Empire."

"Ooooh!" Everyone looked encouragingly at the

King, although he was definitely looking quite dank. His hair was greasy, and he had cockroaches behind his ears (he'd adopted them in exile).

"So what if he's from a Bank Empire? He's still not good enough for a God Queen," Bill hollered triumphantly. "A God Queen needs a strong, spiteful man at her side. A man like me."

"Well, yes, there seems to be a problem with that too. You see, it turns out the Queen is not descended from a family of Gods. She is, in fact, descended from a family of **Gobs**. To put it plainly...

she's a chatter-woman, a gossip, nothing more than a common busybody."

"I always said she was," someone whispered.

CHAPTER EIGHTEEN

DID YOU HEAR THE BELL GO?

"So, what will Brutalia be like now?"

"It'll be a bit like that posho's boat over there that crashed into the spiky shoreline and sank."

"You mean, Brutalia will be under the sea?"

"No, but it'll be a wreck!"

"Want a rat roll, love?"

"No, Mum. For the last time, I'm vegetarian."

"I'll have one, Mrs Canal," Weed said, reaching forward before catching Mort's eye. He snatched his hand back. "On second thoughts, I'm a vegetarian too now."

"Well, Kennet and the kids weren't vegetarian and rat rolls is what they'd want so rat rolls is what we've got."

"Fair enough, Mum," Mort said.

They had gathered on the highest cliff of Brutalia to say their final goodbyes to Kennet and Gosh and Gee. A simple affair, just family, a close friend and a few rat rolls. Punky had given them some heavy rocks that would make a *PLOOF* sound when they hit the water. You needed a symbolic *PLOOF* to put an end to things.

"Sorry about your family," Weed said, linking his arm through Mort's. "Sorry for you too, Mrs Canal."

"What? I was miles away. The neighbours were very rude today, considering it was the funeral. *Stinky sausages, want stinky sausages?* That's what they said. I'll go and bash 'em later." But Mort thought he saw the glitter of tears in his mother's eyes.

Even the excitement of a ding-dong couldn't disguise her pain. Gosh and Gee might have been ratbags who'd rather biff you round the ears than give you a hug, but they were the very best ratbags. And Kennet – he was a good man, and a funny one too. Could make you laugh your rotten potato pie up with one of his rude jokes. They were family.

It was time for the funeral. Avon, Weed and Mort each took a rocky package representing a lost member of the Canal family and rolled it to the cliff edge. With a final shove, the stones plummeted off the lip and down towards that terrible watery graveyard. They strained their ears for the symbolic *PLOOFs* that would symbolize the final goodbye.

PLOOF
"CAREFUL!"
PLOOF
"HANG ON!"
PLOOF
"WATCH IT!"

What! Were the rocks speaking? Was the sea complaining? Why were the *ploofs* so talkative? They flattened their bodies against the ground and peered over the edge to see what was going on below.

"Holy mackerel!" Mort yelped.

For below, in a small boat, was Mort's dad. And behind him were the twins known as Gosh and Gee. Perfectly alive and well, and not looking a bit like overcooked frankfurters.

"Well, bless my cutlery drawer!" exclaimed Avon.

"I don't blimmin' believe it!" Weed shouted.

Mort said nothing. Because nothing could describe the surprise, relief and utter joy that was bouncing round his inner organs like a puppy in a pinball machine.

They were ALIVE!

When they were back on dry land, Kennet and the twins stuffed their faces with the funeral buffet. They were absolutely starving, and it wasn't until every rat roll had been gobbled up, and Gosh and Gee had performed a celebration bash-up with their big brother, that they were ready to do some talking.

Clutching a tugged ear in one hand and a bruised knee in the other, Mort couldn't have been happier. In a jumble of excitement and interruptions, the windswept gang revealed how the waves had plucked them from the rocks; how they were then gobbled whole by a salty mega-shark; how later, deep in the darkness of the beast's belly, Kennet remembered the bottle of **Eau de Errr de Plumber** in his back pocket. A few squirts of that rotten perfume had made the shark vomit them all up – alive, whole, a little bit gunky. But the most terrible part of the story was how, after floating for days on a crate that said EXOTIC BANANAS, they spotted a raft and called for help.

Kennet tutted and growled as he remembered the episode. "They ignored us. Totally ignored us. You can imagine how we felt after everything we'd been through. What a whelk-bum, I said to the kids. What a total and utter—"

Mort leaped to his feet as his father's words brought

back a painful memory. A memory that was clouded by the dark breath of demons, but clearly showed him the image of a distant shipwreck and pants on sticks.

"That was me," he said, his voice cracking. "Oh wow, I really was a total whelk-bum."

"Well, you did save us eventually," Kennet said, squeezing his eldest child affectionately. "We came across a strange bunch – called themselves the Fisherfolk's Cooperative of Luncheon Island. Luncheon Island? Never heard of it. But, Mort, you won't believe it – one of them had a picture of YOUR FACE on his leg. He's a big fan of yours, it turns out. They fed us seafood fit for a god then popped us in a rowing boat. That's how we made it all the way back here to Brutalia."

"That was lucky, Dad," Mort said, wiping a tear from his eye. "But all this has taught me an important lesson – never to let myself be blinded by hate again."

"Very good, Mort," said his mum absent-mindedly, although her thoughts were drifting towards the ding-dong she was going to give the neighbours. And Mort knew it.

Blinded by hate.

"Mum, when you get home, perhaps you should check if the neighbours weren't just being kind and *offering* you some stinky sausages. They are your favourite food after all."

"Who cares? Let's ding-dong anyway!" shouted Gee.

"Why not? We've earned it, right?" said Kennet, kissing his wife's rosy cheek.

"Yeah! You'll help us, won't you, Mort?" said Gosh,tugging at his tunic.

Mort looked at the pleading little rag-bagger-muffin-face and nodded. He couldn't disappoint his brother and sister now – not when they were looking at him so lovingly and being so adorable (despite the hermit crabs in their hair). He'd have to find a way to get out of it later. He always did.

Mort and Weed walked along the rocky cliff edge towards a figure. Punky was silhouetted against the sky – arms thrashing, screaming like a thousand banshees trapped in a pyramid. And, way below, the beautiful Belgo splashed happily in the waves.

"She's amazing, don't you think?"

The squeaky voice came from behind them. It belonged to a grubby little kid called Ferg Futchet, member of a particularly violent street gang of shin-kickers. He was dressed in shredded black clothes and had blood pouring down his neck.

"Ugh! Are you OK?" Mort said, aghast. "Did you get in a fight?"

"Nah, I just pierced my ear with a nail." He gazed at Punky. "I want to be just like her. Lots of us do."

More kids popped up behind him. Some were bleeding; some had mud circles round their eyes. One girl that Mort *knew* was called Ursula said her name was now Urchin; she had collected slug gunk and spiked her hair to look like one. Just like Punky. They gathered by Punky's rock and thrash-danced along to her singing.

"I really hope this isn't going to be the start of something called Punky Rock Music," Weed groaned, sticking his fingers in his ears. "I can't think of anything worse."

"I can," Mort said. "If you keep hate inside, it turns you ugly. It's probably better to get it out."

"That's deep," Weed said, nodding.

Heart songs, hate songs, whatever – so long as it wasn't hurting anyone. In fact, it was a pretty pacifisty way of doing things.

"I think we should talk to Punky about becoming a pacifist," Mort mused. "And, Weed? You've really shone on this adventure – so, from now on, you're a full member of the Pacifist Society of Brutalia."

"But ... but I fought a crab! I punched myself in the face! And I really fancied one of those rat rolls, if I'm honest. I'm not sure I could ever be a proper pacifist."

"We all slip up from time to time. But, Weed, your heart is kind, your words are gentle, and you're the one who showed me the way back, remember?"

"Oh yeah. You were being demonic, unfriendly, vengeful—"

"I get the picture," Mort laughed.

There was a sudden cheer, almost like a group of rock music fans at the end of a concert, and the kids waved so vigorously it made the air move.

And, before you ask, yes, that is how they became known as fans.

And yes, that is how Punk Rock Music was born.

And yes, that is how Punky Mason the rock-crusher found happiness.

"Funny what happens if you give a hater a little love," Weed said wistfully.

They looked back at the rock concert where a particularly strange kind of music – like a mega-shark crunching train tracks – was making a bunch of kids really happy. And the Belgo too. It was so excited it was thrashing its arms and unwittingly flipping nearby ships like cockles in a frying pan.

"Someone's going to get hurt," Weed winced.

"Hmmm. Now that Punky's got a little love, it's time we gave her a little job."

"Crushing rocks?"

"No. One that gives her a sense of purpose."

"What do you mean?" Weed asked, eyes wide with chocolate wonder.

"You'll see."

The next day, Mort and Weed strolled through Brutalia. It was grubbing up again nicely after its uncharacteristic clean. Everyone agreed it really wasn't right for the island to be so shiny and spotless. It just wasn't home. So all the citizens lent hands, buckets of slop and piles of poo to scrub all traces of ~~beautiful~~ right out of it. Olfa Smelch even donated bottles of his **Eau de Errr** as air-unfreshener. (And yes, that is where the word ODOUR comes from.)

"It'll be good when everything's back to normal," Weed said. "When the backstreets and side streets are revolting once more, and when the King is back from his holiday 'to think things over' in the Exotics. I hope he'll take her back."

"If he loves cockroaches as much as he seems to, she's got a chance," Mort said.

"I wonder if the Queen's going to be OK after her embarrassment. Not that there's anything wrong with being from a family of street-corner gossips..."

"I know what you mean, Mort. It's just a bit of a

step down from being a God."

"And you should know, oh great Weather God."

"Very funny, Weed," Mort said, nudging his friend.

"Must have been fun, though, being a god for a while."

"It felt a bit stressful actually," Mort said with a sad smile. "Imagine living your life with everyone expecting you to be something you're not."

"Like Punky?"

"Yes, like Punky. Although she knows who she is now. A pacifist, just like us."

"Nice one, Mort."

"Thanks, Weed. Shall we go dangle our feet off the docks and watch the sunset?"

The boys raced down to the docks and sat on the rickety planks. It was all quiet apart from the slap of the sea and the yell of the ravens, which circled above, hoping a posho had fallen overboard and there'd be washed-up eyeballs for tea.

Weed tugged Mort's tunic and pointed. At the far end of the docks was a lobster – one of the lucky ones – and he was studiously practising his cha-cha-cha. One, two, kick!

Mort and Weed hid their laugh behind their hands and swung their legs over the docks, ready to plunge them into those cutting salty waters. When—

Dung-a-lung-a-lung-lung!
And it wasn't saucepans in a squall...

"Did the bell go?" Weed asked.

"Yes," Mort smiled. "The Belgo."

The boys quickly pulled their feet clear of the water. High up on a rock, Punky continued to ring out her warning to Brutalia's ships. **The Belgo is coming! The Belgo is coming!** Because this was her new job, her purpose, her pride: to make sure this magnificent creature of the Salty Sea was never misunderstood again (and to warn nearby ships in case they accidently got hurled slung, suckered and sunk).

"What are you doing, Mort?" Weed asked.

Mort had picked up a perfectly round limpet shell and was scratching white lines into the slate-grey surface. "Punky asked me to design her a tattoo as a memento of our adventures, so that's what I'm doing."

"But what is it?"

"It's supposed to be the Belgo. The head and the three legs, see?"

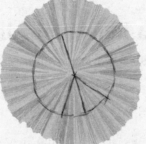

"The head isn't right at all. You're not very good at drawing, Mort."

"It's not supposed to be realistic. It's symbolic of the Belgo. In fact, I think it's quite striking. Tell you what, it could be our sign, Weed. Our sign for peace."

"Can we stick them on ravens?"

"If they stay still long enough," Mort said.

Weed and Mort imagined spreading peace across the spiky land of Brutalia. It was an urchin of an island, but it had a soft centre – it was well hidden, but it was there. After all, who would have thought a brutal rock-crusher could become a protector of life?

As the light faded, they fell silent. While Weed thought whatever he was thinking, Mort looked back at all the times he'd nearly given up, thinking that there'd never be a place for his Pacifist Society on this ugly island. But there was – there *really* was. And now it was three members strong. If there was anything that Punky and the Belgo had taught him, it was that calling something ugly or horrible just because you don't understand it is bad for everyone. Because there is magnificence in existence and beauty wherever you look for it.

Mort skimmed a shell across the water and smiled as ripples broke through the reflection of the peachy sky, which had turned the grey sea into a blushing pool. And, as the round orange sun fizzled on the horizon, the glowing dome of the Belgo bobbed beneath it and then disappeared beneath the waves. With a very happy *ploof.*

THE END

ACKNOWLEDGEMENTS

Huge thanks to my right-hand team (some of whom are left-handed): Alice Williams, my wonderful agent; Anni and Michael Delahaye – marvellous humans who happen to be my parents (which is an incredible coincidence); and my friends, who lift me up. Especially Beverly Caston, Hattie Bosnell, Vanessa Ferret and Lucy Wendover, who have given me untold Mort support.

Thank you also to my writing network. Too many to name them all, but I will mention Gareth P Jones, Tom Easton, Jo Nadin and Martin Howard, who keep me buoyant on these rocky seas.

Darling Matilda and Ben, thank you for reminding me not to take life too seriously (because you sure as hell don't). And Mike, I'm forever grateful to you for giving me the freedom and space to create. It's invaluable.

I'm hugely indebted to Little Tiger, who not only believed in *Mort the Meek*, but have now helped a second story wriggle out of the boggy backstreets of Brutalia into the wider world. Mattie, Thy, Charlie and the team: you're the best. And of course, I must thank the amazing George Ermos for his hilarious, eye-popping illustrations that bring the words to life.

Most of all I want to thank the kids and adults who read these books. You must be mad, but I am very glad you are.

Rachel Delahaye was born in Australia but
has lived in the UK since she was six years old.
She studied linguistics and worked as a magazine
writer and editor before becoming a children's author.
Rachel loves reading, cooking and wandering about
in woodlands. Somewhere in between all that she
writes. She especially enjoys writing comedy and says,
profoundly: Life without comedy is like cereal
without milk – dry and hard to swallow.

Rachel has two lively children and a dog called Rocket,
and lives in the beautiful city of Bath.

George Ermos is an illustrator, maker and avid
reader from England. He works digitally and enjoys
illustrating all things curious and mysterious.